Nila
PRINCESS OF SHEBA

MUKAMI NGARI

First Published in Great Britain in 2024 by
LOVE AFRICA PRESS
103 Reaver House, 12 East Street, Epsom KT17 1HX
www.loveafricapress.com

LOVE AFRICA
PRESS
African Love Stories

Blurb

Enter the land of Sheba in this first book of the Star Summoner series.

Love. Sacrifice, Betrayal.

As the first-born daughter of the grand emperor of Sheba, Nila knows of her father's ambitions to conquer the empires of the highlands. She does not share in his dream but she will do anything he asks to protect her sisters, including betray her true love, Prince Seni of Kitara.

Disgraced, Seni plots to take his empire back, and get his revenge on Nila. With so much at stake, the only option is to win.

There is going to be a war in the highlands, and Nila and Seni will face each other in their darkest forms. This might be the end for both, unless the fiery passion between them consumes them first.

*The records of the Star Summoner's life
are kept in the vaults
of the celestial city of Nahu.*

Prologue

"What is taking her so long? Surely, it can't be that hard!"

As Emperor Nefe of Sheba paces around his expansive throne room, his exasperated sighs make the room feel small and brew more anxiety in the twelve kings from the twelve provinces of Sheba who've gathered around their emperor in the midnight hour.

"It's her first time, and from what I've heard, childbirth is quite taxing on a woman's body," King Mesati of Astabara replies.

He's unfortunately been chosen by the other kings as their mouthpiece tonight, and he has to attend to the emperor's whims, risking his wrath at every turn. They usually do this when he is in one of his unpredictable moods.

Once when he was in such a mood, he'd ordered King Wosasi of Asoasa flogged for accidentally calling him emperor, instead of

'Grand Emperor' as he preferred. So King Mesati knows he has to be careful with his words and actions tonight, or it will be his turn to be humiliated.

"It has taken all day, and it's now close to midnight," the grand emperor complains as he gobbles down all the wine in his shining gold chalice and snaps his fingers at the wine bearer standing by the door. The young, dark-skinned man in blue velvet pants and coat, the uniform of the palace servants, rushes forward carrying a gold flask in both hands and refills the emperor's chalice.

"I believe it's been exceptionally long because it's a mage. Mages take longer." King Mesati squeezes the grand emperor's shoulder. A blatant liar is what he's become to appease his master. He wishes upon the stars of Nahu, the celestial city, that it isn't a mage.

"Soon, you will hold him in your arms, and you will forget all about this long night, Grand Emperor," King Mesati declares as another sharp scream pierces through the night from the midwife's chambers, where Teshat, the emperor's companion, is giving birth.

"Wine," the grand emperor commands as he plops down on his throne made with pure gold from the Asoasa region, engraved with a roaring lion, fangs on display, and a crown on its mane. The wine bearer runs along the black and white marble floor and refills the chalice.

"It has to be…it has to be." The emperor's eyes are wild as he looks at King Mesati. The first seed he's planted in his wife has to be a mage. He married Teshat because she was of the Kanji bloodline, the powerful male mages who once ruled the highlands for centuries.

The last eight generations of Kanji males had been born without magic, but he figured there was a chance Teshat could give him a mage. A child, a son with her blood, will be powerful, and if that power is put to good use, he'll expand the empire of Sheba to the ends of the world.

Teshat's screams stop. When the child's first cry reaches his ears, the emperor stands on his feet, flings his chalice away, and gathers his cloak around his shoulders. On his way out, he pushes aside King Mesati who bumps into the wine bearer and knocks down the flask, the red contents inside it spilling on the marble floor.

"Forgive me, Grand Emperor," the wine bearer apologizes profusely as he bends and begins wiping the floor with his blue velvet coat—the emperor cannot fathom stains on his black and white checkered floor.

"Perhaps we should wait for the midwife to call for us, Grand Emperor," King Mesati reasons as he follows behind the emperor, who is hurrying out of his throne room, the floor groaning where his black leather boots step. The other kings follow a few paces behind, each praying the stars will not let the child be a mage.

"Flaming stars! Enough of your coddling Mesati. I've endured it all night. Shut. Up!"

The grand emperor walks upstairs to the last room on the east wing overlooking the trickling water pond. It has a salt lick, and at around midday, his zebras which roam on the palace grounds pass by here to drink water. This room has the best view of the beautiful creatures. He is the only one who uses it, but today, he's allowed Teshat to use it since she went into labour.

After all, she has finally done something worthwhile with her life—she is birthing him his heir. His guard, Nasou, a giant of a man who stands at seven feet, tries the latch on the door; it's locked.

"The grand emperor wishes to come in," he alerts Kaku, the midwife. There is no answer, but they can hear Kaku's whispers and the sharp cry of the emperor's newborn.

"Kick it down," Emperor Nefe commands Nasou as he balls his fists. He will have the midwife lashed for keeping him waiting out in the dark. Her work is done, the child is out, and there is no explanation for her delay except for insolence.

Nasou kicks the heavy mahogany door down from its hinges, and it falls back with a loud bang. The emperor and his kings walk in.

"Grand Emperor, she needs to be sewn and cleaned. I need a little more—"

Before Kaku can finish speaking, Nasou pushes her aside. The midwife, who is holding blood-soaked rags in her hands, steps away. The entourage brushes past her towards the new mother and child.

"Forgive me, Grand Emperor," Teshat whispers.

She is lying on the bloody bed, sweat and tears pouring down her face and on her quivering lips. The lamp beside her flickers, and on the walls, her shadow looks like a young tree bent by a mighty wind until it touches the ground and is about to snap in half.

The child she has birthed is curled beside her. Mages are born with black soles on their feet. This one does not have black soles, and as if that is not enough, it is a girl. She has long limbs, a head full of tiny ringlet curls, and a heart-shaped face. Her eyes are closed, and her head turns in her mother's direction, trying with all her might to reach her with her balled fists.

"She needs to suckle." Kaku hands the child to its mother.

Teshat refuses to touch the crying girl and looks away at the wall to hide her face in shame. The girl is bundled up in bleached white furs. The emperor had hunted down the white fox himself in the forests of Astabara together with his guards for two whole days. He'd presented them to a pregnant Teshat as a gift for his heir.

Kaku shushes the child in her arms as she gives her some sugared water, which the girl suckles on and drifts to sleep.

When the grand emperor's left eye twitches and he chuckles as if something is stuck in his throat, King Mesati senses the sweet girl does not have long in this world.

"Grand Emperor Nefe, it is an auspicious night. If it pleases my wise emperor, perhaps you might ask Tesfaye, the chief astrologer, to read her stars."

Kaku nods, agreeing with King Mesati. She bows her head, eyes on the emperor's boots, hoping he cannot see her flaring nostrils and the anger in her eyes. She is not good at hiding her emotions, unlike the people at the emperor's court. Her back hurts. Teshat's labour lasted twenty-one long hours, during none of which Kaku had the time to sit down and rest her feet. On top of that, she had to answer to the meddling emperor every turn of the hour by reporting to him in his throne room, as well as endure his threats in the process. It had been the most tense she'd been at a birth, and she'd overseen hundreds of births for over ten years.

"Very well, then," Grand Emperor Nefe barks. "Summon him immediately. Hurry."

Kaku looks around. Where will she keep the child? She does not trust leaving her with her parents, but she cannot go outside with her. The cold might seep into her skin and her delicate organs. She knows many people who would do anything to hold a child of their own, but the gods have looked the other way and forgotten their empty wombs and their expectant waiting arms. How can the emperor and his wife not realise how blessed they are?

"Let me." King Mesati takes the sleeping girl in his arms. He stands by the window and faces away from the emperor, shielding the newborn from his rising anger.

"Please let her live," Kaku beseeches the stars as she sprints across the field to where the servants of the palace live, in small houses leaning against each other in a circle, all of them the colour of damp ash.

As it is late in the night, most of them are fast asleep, but she can see a few lamps burning in some of the rooms. She walks past the houses to the rocks near the kitchen where they make the palace's food. The air here always smells like freshly baked bread and lamb, roast meat and curry stews, meals fit for an emperor.

"Chief astrologer, the emperor summons you to the palace," she says, stumbling over the words.

Tesfaye is lying on the rocks, facing the sky, gazing at the stars, like he does every night. He is a strange man. He rarely talks to anyone, but she loves the way he walks, back straight, hands beside him, regal, like a king.

"The child, it's not a mage, then?" he asks, still gazing at the stars in the moonlight sky. She often wonders if he can see Nahu, the celestial city.

"Yes, but she's a healthy, strong girl."

Tesfaye stands up, picks up his star map, and adjusts the blue turban on his head. The orbs of his eyes glow luminous white.

They hurry back to the palace, and before they walk up the flight of stairs to the upper room, Kaku turns to Tesfaye. "Her life is in your hands."

"I only say what the stars tell me to say. I cannot lie, Kaku," Tesfaye declares.

"Sometimes, it's necessary to lie for the better good," Kaku says as she narrows her eyes at him.

She'd heard he is a man of principle, but she can't believe he'll let the child die, all because he can't tell a simple lie.

"I apologize. I cannot do what you ask of me."

Damn his principles, and to think she finds him attractive. She feels a tightening in her chest as he opens the door.

"Grand Emperor." Tesfaye bows as they walk inside.

The grand emperor is sitting on a chair near the open door. The newborn child, whose fate now hung in the balance, remains quiet in King Mesati's arms as if she senses the impending doom.

Tesfaye takes a look at the sleeping newborn in King Mesati's arms. He never lies about what the stars say, and he won't begin today.

"Ah, yes. Here it is." He runs his fingers across the map, searching for the constellation of stars that match the one in tonight's sky. "The girl is born under the realm of the archer. The celestial city of Nahu smiles upon us, on this day of her birth. The stars declare that she will save the empire." Then he folds his map and puts it back in his robe. "That is all, Grand Emperor."

Tesfaye bows and takes his leave. The grand emperor looks at the girl.

"What a precious gift from the celestial city, indeed," King Mesati says as he smiles. He hands the girl to the emperor who holds her for a brief moment and gives her to Kaku. Then, he stomps out of the room, King Mesati and the other kings trailing behind.

"Should we congratulate him, then?" King Wosasi asks as he struggles to catch up. He is short and heavy, a consequence of his love for fat steak.

"If you want your head to roll, then yes." They stand at the entrance of the throne room as they watch the emperor who is already inside, roaring with the rage of a captured bull. He flings his chalice at the wall.

"The Grand Emperor wishes to be alone," Nasou informs the kings as he shuts the massive doors of the throne room with the help of three guards.

As King Mesati walks towards his courtyard, he rubs the temples of his aching head. It has been another long day, but he's survived, and the girl has lived.

He greatly misses Astabara. He misses his six-year-old son, Barane, and his queen, Serafi. He hasn't been home in three years. The emperor has ordered the kings of Sheba to stay in the palace, for fear they might insight uprisings in their kingdoms. He trusts no one, and so he's reduced them to ceremonial figureheads. All their movements are watched and reported to him.

But the girl has lived. It is not yet her time to meet the Nahuiri, also known as the ascendants who help the souls of all to cross to Nahu. If she's survived today, then she'll survive anything.

"Let it be so," he implores the stars.
***

"Her name shall be Nila," the grand emperor declares to his kings in the throne room.

It is three days after the girl's birth, and according to the thousand-year-old scrolls from the celestial city, this is when a soul is ready to begin its mortal journey.

If it had been a mage, a boy, he'd have named him Nefe the Fifth. He desperately needs a magical heir, and now that Teshat's womb is empty, they will start trying again, immediately, starting tonight.

"You are now in the presence of the Grand Emperor of Sheba, the unconquered mighty sting."

Piayu, the royal announcer startles the emperor from his thoughts. The man's voice sounds like thunder during a heavy storm.

"Tesfaye, what brings you?" the emperor asks as the chief astrologer bows before him. The last time he saw him was when he declared the girl would save the empire.

He knows the stars never lie, but he finds it hard to believe that about a mere girl.

"Grand Emperor."

Tesfaye unfolds his scrolls. His glowing eyes unnerve Emperor Nefe. No man should hold such power except for him.

"I read the stars on your behalf as I do every night, and they say that...they say..."

"Flaming stars, Tesfaye, say it already. I don't have all day," the grand emperor says as he snaps his fingers at the wine bearer. "Is it about the girl?"

"No, it's not about the girl...it's about you. It says that the crown upon your head shall fall if you set your sights on Aksa, the first empire."

"I see," the emperor says as he takes a sip of his wine and swirls his chalice around.

He is tired of the chief astrologer and his bloody stars. He's had enough of waiting upon the stars to determine what he should do in his life. He will forge his path. Nothing will stand in his way of conquering Aksa, the so-called first empire, no matter how long it takes. If only he could find the book of Aksa which has all the knowledge one needs to know about the empire.

No one knows what Aksa looks like on the inside. The empire is surrounded by long, high, impenetrable walls that reach to the skies. The rulers never respond to diplomatic invites, and they never invite anyone into the empire. They keep to themselves, their borders closed to the rest of the highlands. They didn't trade with anyone, which means they were self-sufficient.

Outsiders who try to go in are promptly executed by their lethal archers who stand guard on top of the high walls, hidden by the skies. One can't see them, but they can see you. No one has ever made it inside.

Whatever they have in Aksa is good.

The emperor imagines it has caves filled with gold, and there is a lot he can do with that kind of wealth. He'll forge weapons and build a formidable army. Conquer lands from Sheba to Kerma. He'll even rule across the Qeyhlil Sea in Araba.

As part of his plan, he's found Kaba, the beady-eyed wizard from the mystery schools of Kerma who understands his vision and shares in it. They'll wait together until Teshat births him a mage, and Kaba will teach the boy how to wield magic. He'll be strong enough to bring down the walls of Aksa.

On his part, the emperor will continue his search for the book so they'll know as much as he could about the first empire.

He sighs, his eye twitching as the chief astrologer closes his scrolls. There is a burning in his chest and a desire to see the man's head roll. He wonders if his eyes will still glow then.

"Long live the Grand Emperor," Tesfaye excuses himself and leaves the throne room. From the smug grin on the emperor's face, his head will soon roll. He has to leave Sheba, his land of birth, all because he cannot tell a lie.

He runs into Kaku in the palace hallway. She is carrying herbs in her basket for Teshat who is still recovering from childbirth.

He loves how diligent she is in her work, and how she cares for the new mothers and their children. He's enamoured by her calm voice and her easy smile, but he's never dared to tell her so. It is now or never.

"Let me help," he offers towards the basket.

"Thank you." Kaku offers him the handle, and their fingers brush against each other.

He walks her up to Teshat's room. She's been moved from the airy upper room back to her quarters in the east wing of the palace.

"I'm leaving Sheba, you should come with me," he says when they get to the door. Inside, the girl cries, and Kaku's brows are lifted with worry.

16

"Nila has no one…she needs me," Kaku says as she takes back the basket.

Tesfaye nods, understanding this is who Kaku is—a protector, a nurturer.

"Farewell, Tesfaye."

He memorizes her face like he does constellations and stores it in the depths of his soul, then watches as she opens the door and goes inside.

He waits in his room until midnight and then sneaks into the horse stables and flees on a black stallion. He doesn't know where to go, but he follows the stars because the stars never lie.

Chapter One

I've been summoned.

I stand outside the throne room and wait. Two guards open the enormous gold doors and let me in. I walk inside, my footsteps echoing on the marble floor. I don't come here often, only when I've gotten myself into trouble. But I've been too busy lately—I haven't got the time to get in trouble.

"You are now in the presence of the Grand Emperor Nefe of Sheba, the unconquered mighty sting," Piayu, the royal announcer declares, as I approach my papo on his throne.

King Mesati sits on Papo's right. He winks at me, and I smile. Kaba, the wizard, sits on Papo's left, and he narrows his eyes at me. The man hates me. I don't know what I ever did to him.

"Papo." I bow. "I trust the preparations for the Nefe games are going well?"

"Since when are you interested in the Nefe games?" he asks, his brow lifting.

A month from now, the Nefe games, which he named after himself, will be happening. I hate them. Apart from the common games like sword fighting, blade throwing, wrestling, and shooting arrows, the Nefe games also involve bare fights with the Kilishi.

I've heard Papo talk proudly about the Kilishi to his guests many times. "At first, they look like deceivingly small jackals, with their usual black and golden coats, but would you believe that little body contains the strength of a stallion? Do you see those needle-sized spikes on its skin? They hold the venom of a desert scorpion, and the claws where its feet used to be can tear through flesh and bone."

They are hideous creatures modified with dark magic by the wizard Kaba. I've never seen anyone face them and live.

"I love the games. I always have." I smile.

He sighs, eyeing me as he lifts his wine chalice to his lips. "All invitations have been sent out, and all the emperors of the highlands and their royal households have confirmed that they are coming except for Aksa."

"That was expected," I say as I shrug. The emperor of Aksa, which is also known as the first empire, usually never responds to such invites. Nothing has changed this year.

According to the map in Papo's throne room, Sheba lies in the Far East, Bazina and Pemba are in the middle, Iteri and Deome are in the South,

Aksa is in the West, and Areppata and Nagarim lie in the North. The map has every detail of the other empires, but Aksa is blank. All we know is they have high walls all around their borders, walls that reach up to the clouds in the skies.

"Enough with the questions, Nila. I've summoned you here to let you know that I've found a worthy suitor for you, and this time, I don't want to hear any of your excuses. This match is happening," Papo declares.

Chapter Two

Not again. I thought he'd given up on this quest. I'm twenty, and he's been trying to marry me off since I turned fifteen. I've managed to scare away every suitor he's found for me. In my defense, he is not good at choosing suitors.

"I've lost allies because of your behaviour, Nila. You have humiliated me enough. This time, it's happening. You are getting married," Papo says as he stares me down.

"Who is it?" I rub my chin, already thinking of how to frighten this one away. I might have to lie to him that I have a tail—it works every time. It has worked on princes, warriors, and merchants, all members of esteemed families which Papo has tried to forge alliances with.

"Prince Eshi of Kush."

My blood chills. The Prince Eshi he is talking about is widely known as a slave master. He travels across the empires and purchases men, women, and children like cattle. He herds them together like animals and transports them across the Qeyhlil Sea to Araba, where they are forced to work in the desert sun for the rest of their lives.

I don't think Prince Eshi would run away if I told him I had a tail. I think it would excite him; pain excites him. I've seen him twice at the Nefe games cheering at the top of his lungs as Kilishi tore men from limb to limb. Whenever he visits Sheba, I make sure to stay as far away from him as possible.

"I won't marry him." I stand my ground.

"I've already decided that you will, and if you refuse, then your sister Sahara will marry him, or Nakai, or Etana, or Makeda," he threatens.

I stand straight. He knows this will catch my full attention to the seriousness of the matter.

Prince Eshi must be offering a really good dowry because that's all Papo cares about, dowry.

"My sisters won't marry him, too," I add. Sahara is eighteen, Nakai is fifteen, Etana is thirteen, and Makeda is seven.

"Nila, I have already decided. You have no say in this matter," he barks.

It takes all the strength inside me not to flee. When his tone sounds like this, he might have me lashed. It won't be the first time.

"How much is he offering to pay you? I'll pay it," I blurt out.

I am in charge of the commerce of spices and oils. I oversee their planting, harvest, storage, and trade. I work closely with three thousand farmers across the empire. We mostly trade across the highlands in cloves, basil, and cinnamon, and as for oils, Sheba's myrrh is the best.

Our current annual income is three hundred thousand coins in bronze and a hundred thousand in gold. It is negligent compared to what the empire gets in the trade of gold and fabric, but it is something.

If I expand our trade routes across the highlands, then I can pay off this dowry, and then he'll leave me alone. He'll leave my sisters alone, and we'll have a say as to who we choose to marry. We will marry for love, like the princesses in the stories Nakai loves to read.

"Nila, do you know what you are saying?"

"I'll pay you whatever he is offering to give. I'll also pay my sisters' dowries' and you will leave us alone." By the stars of the Nahu, I'll do it.

I can hear the deafening silence in the throne room. King Mesati stares at me as if I've lost my mind. The frown on Kaba's face remains the same, and Papo narrows his eyes at me.

"Papo, all I ask is that you give me a year, and I'll pay this dowry. If I'm not done by then, you can do as you choose. A year is all I ask for."

"Nila," he snaps at me, tapping his boots on his footstool.

"Twelve months, Papo. That's all I need. So tell me how much Prince Eshi was going to pay you..."

"He offered to bring me the book of Aksa as your dowry."

Chapter Three

I blink fast. Papo's wanted to get his hands on the damn book of Aksa for as long as I can remember. He wants to know as much as he can about the secluded first empire.

"That is impossible!" I argue. "You do realize he is lying to you."

"Careful, girl. Are you calling me a fool?"

"No, I'm just saying that it's impossible, Papo." I lower my voice and my gaze.

"I don't have to explain myself to you, but if you must know, Prince Eshi is returning from his journey in Araba in less than two months, and he says he's found a way to get me the book, and much more." He sighs.

"I will get you the book of Aksa." I square my shoulders. I know how much he wants this. "But if I give it to you, it's not only my dowry that's paid off but my sisters', as well," I say as I tap my foot.

I don't even know where to start looking, but I'll find the damn book. I will do whatever I must to not marry Eshi and to set my sisters free from the same fate.

"Forgive me, Grand Emperor, "Piayu interrupts. "I've just been informed that you have received a message from Aksa."

Papo and I stare at Piayu.

"Read it," Papo says as he sits upright on his throne.

I believe this is the first message anyone has ever received from inside Aksa.

"It says that the Emperor and Empress of Aksa, together with the Crown Prince, will attend the Nefe games," Piayu says.

I take the note from Piayu's hands and read it, then hand it over to Papo. He remains silent for a few moments as his eyes roam over the note.

"The emperor, the empress, and the crown prince." Papo looks at the note for a long time then he stands and walks towards me. He stares at me and shakes his head. "Nila, I think you might succeed on this quest. You won't get the book, technically, but it will be the same as if you got the book. You must succeed, you will succeed." His eyes seem determined.

"I will?" I ask. I don't even know where to begin.

"I think you stand a chance, so I'll give you a head start," he says, patting my head.

"You will?"

"Yes. But it will come at a cost. You will follow my orders, no argument."

"I accept." I'll take whatever help I can get even if it's from the master of devious games himself.

"Good. You will begin your training with Dalia immediately. Go wait for her in your room," he says as he turns me around until I face the door. He walks back to his throne. End of conversation.

Dalia? What will his mistress teach me about the book of Aksa?

She is a stunning dark brown-skinned woman. Most of the time, she wears a scandalous red silk dress that exposes her cleavage, with a long slit ending mid-thigh. She has a wasp-sized waist and curvy hips. She looks like the goddess of fertility. She rarely walks around in the palace and sticks to her quarters which Papo built for her in the west tower. When Papo is not in the throne room, rest assured he is with her.

Ten minutes later, I'm pacing around my room when Dalia walks in. Her feet spring on the floor. She moves like a cat on the hunt.

A young kitchen maid follows behind her. She is wearing a long green dress and a matching scarf covered in grease and soot. She is carrying a bucket of water on her head, which she pours in my tub and leaves. Then, she comes back with a basket filled with an assortment of things—I see a jar of honey, lemons, oils, and jars of butter, as well as two large flasks. She places the basket beside my tub as Dalia, who has been silently staring at me, gets closer to me.

She examines my face, turning it left and right.

"You know, I've seen you around the palace. You are a beautiful girl, the brown skin, big eyes, and full lips." She walks around me, sizing me up. "The thick hair in a bun and the curves, but there is a lot that needs to be fixed."

"I thought we were here because you're supposed to help me get the book of Aksa."

She ignores me as she walks around me again. "Open your mouth," she demands.

"This is ridiculous." I bare my teeth at her. "Not to mention a waste of my time."

"No missing teeth. Good, this makes my work easier. But why are they so yellow? We have to fix that immediately," She inspects my neck and collarbone. "Good. No more going out in the sun until I tell you so."

She walks towards the tub and picks a jar of honey from the basket brought by the kitchen maid. She pours all the sticky liquid in the bath, then she picks one of the flasks and pours milk inside. The next flask also contains milk, and she pours all of it inside before mixing everything with her hands.

"Who are you to tell me such things?" She makes no sense, and I'm already tired of her.

"The grand emperor said you should obey everything I say, or do you wish to disobey him? Clothes off, get in here." She points at the tub.

"What exactly are you supposed to teach me, how to take a bath? I know how to take a bath." This is getting out of hand, and I feel insulted she'd even dare to tell me such a thing.

"Get in the water, and stay there until I come back," she says, pursing her lips at me.

Chapter Four

When she leaves, I head to the archives, a lonely grey edifice built in the far west of the palace. This is where the empire's record keepers are situated.

"Princess?" The young kitchen girl follows behind. She is carrying lemons and a scrubbing cloth in her basket. "The mistress said I should scrub the turmeric stains from your fingers."

"You will do no such thing. Leave me alone." I feel bad for yelling at her, but I've changed my mind, and I want no part in whatever weird training Papo and his mistress have in mind for me. No walking in the sun? What is that about?

She scurries back, and I do not stop walking until I reach the archives. The record keeper on duty is Mari, and no one is more knowledgeable than she is. She was of great help when I was mapping out the routes we would use to trade spices across the highlands. I know she will point me in the right direction about this damn book.

"Nila, it's been a while," Mari says as she lets me in. The last time I was here, she'd almost thrown me out for eating a piece of bread in the archives. I'd spent all day in the spice barns and I was hungry, so I'd snuck in bread, but Mari was not having it. This is a sacred space to her.

"I need your help," I say as I look around the rows of scrolls and records.

I see Dalia and Nasou, the giant guard, coming towards the archives, and she has a grin on her perfect face.

"You can take the bath yourself. Considering the work you do, it seems like you need it more than I do," I say to Dalia as I scroll through records.

"I was hoping you would disobey me," Dalia says as she smiles.

Her teeth are the whitest I've ever seen. Nasou drags me by my wrist, and I try to get out of his grasp and fail. We all head back to my room, and Dalia closes the door behind us.

"Take these rags off her body," she instructs as she sits on my bed and crosses her legs.

I sink my nails into Nasou's face and arms as he rips the linen dress from my body and dumps it on the ground. I cover my exposed breasts with my hands. I've never felt so humiliated in my life.

"You can't do this to me. Wait till I tell Papo," I say as I ball my fists.

I hate the sight of blood, but I will enjoy seeing their two heads roll on the black and white floor of the throne room. There is no way Papo asked them to do this to me. I look at the trunk of clothes near my bed—it holds a dagger inside. I won't hesitate to use it if they dare try anything.

"Silly little princess." Dalia chuckles as she stands up. "Nasou, get her in the water."

He grabs me and submerges me in the tub. The cold water bites into my skin.

"Keep her there until I come back," she says as she leaves.

I struggle to free myself, but Nasou holds me in place by pressing down on my shoulders.

"You will regret this," I warn. His stone face remains unmoved.

I stay in the water for so long, my whole body grows numb, and my teeth are chattering. The kitchen girl comes back with her basket and kneels beside the tub. She takes my left hand and begins rubbing a lemon on my fingernails. My lips quiver. I take two baths a day; I don't see the need for this unnecessary embarrassing exercise.

Dalia comes back with a basket filled with bottles of oils. "Every morning at sunrise, you will get in the water. Then, we will layer your dry skin first with oil, then butter, then more oil."

She hands me a white linen sheet, and I wrap it around myself as I get out of the water. Nasou and the kitchen girl leave. Dalia applies an oil on my back, then lathers it with butter and then more oil.

"Out of the seven languages in the highlands, how many of them can you speak?"

"All of them," I say as I tighten the linen sheet around my body. I learn new languages easily.

"Mph... I'm shocked, you don't seem well-educated."

She raises a brow. I bite my lip as I'm too tired to retort.

"Your voice is too shrill. I will train you to purr." She applies the oils on my hands. "You stand like a man, and you have hair everywhere." She makes a face, disgusted by my unshaved armpits.

"Careful, mistress," I warn. She is treading on my nerves. I look at the trunk of clothes again. I'm so close to it now, I could reach for my dagger and stab her in her shaved armpits. I'd love to hear what she'd say about it. She always has something to say.

"Unclench your jaw. That frown makes you look old," she commands.

"So what?"

"Blunt and tactless...uneducated in the art of femininity," she reprimands.

"Really, what is it to you? I don't know how any of this will help me get the book." I'm this close to punching her nose.

"Don't play coy with me, Nila. You are a wise young woman. You know what we are doing here. You know there is power in femininity, and I'm fashioning you into the ultimate weapon. If you listen to me, you won't have to fight to get this book of Aksa with daggers and knives. If you listen to me, you will succeed on your quest without breaking a sweat," she says, closing the jar of the scented butter she was applying on me.

I roll my eyes as I sit on my bed. I do know what she means, but growing up, the most feminine woman I knew was my mother. When I was a little girl, I was smitten by how beautiful she was, how soft she spoke, and the beautiful silks she wore. But what did that get her? Nothing. I do not want to end up like her, so I resist this feminine path as much as I can.

When Dalia leaves, I'm finally alone, and I think about how strange the day has been. The sole of my left foot hurts. The kitchen maid, whose name I'd learned was Neret, had scrubbed at it too hard.

"I'm sorry, Princess, there is a stain that won't come out," she'd said as she rubbed a lemon on it and scrubbed until I'd pulled away.

"Forget it, it won't come out." The stain she was trying to remove was a black patch that appeared on my sole a few months ago. It is the size of a coin. I've tried to scrub it away myself and failed. But it doesn't hurt, so I leave it alone.

Chapter Five

It's been almost four weeks of Dalia's lessons. We are done for the day, and I lie on the bed, exhausted, every part of my body slick from all the oil she's applied on me.

I'm not feeling well today. Maybe it's because I haven't been out in the sun for so long. I feel sick. I miss the heat of the sun on my face and the aroma of the spices in the barns.

Mari still hasn't found any records on the book of Aksa, and now, I have eleven months left on the wager I made with Papo.

Suddenly, my door opens wide open and my four sisters, Sahara, Nakai, Etana, and Makeda burst in. They've received the dresses they are to wear at the Nefe games from the dressmaker, and they are excited to show me. The games are happening in three days. I get out of bed and flop on the chair next to my window. I wish I was alone so I could sulk in peace.

"Nila, what do you think of this one? I think it's a little loose around the waist." Sahara twirls as she looks at herself in the full-length mirror in my room.

"You look amazing."

"That dress is perfect," Nakai says in a singing voice. She has the most beautiful voice I've ever heard in my life. When she sings, it feels like a ray of sun on damp skin after a long rain.

"We are going to meet so many princes," Etana says. She is all dreamy-eyed as she looks at herself in the mirror next to Sahara. She loves stories about dashing princes and beautiful princesses, and she often disappears into the archives to read such stories.

"One day, I'll get to participate in the horse racing," Makeda says as she stares at me with big, round eyes which make me forget my troubles.

"Of course." I smile, patting her chubby cheek. At the age of seven, she is a better horse rider than I am.

The next morning, I overhear two servants' chatter as I walk down the palace hallways from the archives. Dalia says I need beauty sleep, but I spend all nights in the archives in the hopes I'll find something on this book. What she doesn't know won't hurt her.

"All the envoys have arrived except for Aksa...I hear their soldiers have already arrived to make sure the place is secure before the emperor and the empress arrive later in the evening," the servant on my left says.

There is a flurry of activity going on throughout the palace. Sheba's official blue flags have been hoisted all over the fields where the games will be taking place tomorrow.

I bump into the kitchen staff as they hurry along with bowls of fruit, plates of meat, and flasks filled with wine, to serve the royal households who've arrived and are staying in the guest quarters. I dash into the kitchens and meet Neret who has a food basket ready for me.

"Thank you," I say before heading out.

Over the past four weeks, we've become friends, and she is an easy-going girl. She's getting married to one of the stable boys in a few weeks. They are in love, and he waits for her outside my door every day before they walk hand in hand to the servants' quarters.

In the food basket is a bowl of stew and bread, and a basket of assorted fruits like grapes, bananas, and apples for Kaku who has been up all night helping one of the kitchen maids give birth.

I open the door of her room with the key she gave me. All my sisters have a key, too. I find her lying on top of her bed, her face buried in the white linen sheets of her bed, her sandals still on her feet. She groans as she sits up, fatigue etched all over her face.

"You have to eat something. I know you last ate yesterday morning." She's always been like a mother to my sisters and me, and I do all I can to take care of her in return.

"Nila, you didn't have to do this. I was about to go to the kitchens." She dips a piece of the bread in the stew and swallows. "Delicious. Did you get this from your Papo's table?"

"Only the best for you." I smile as I pour her some water from the flask on the table. "I keep saying you need a servant assigned to you, someone to make sure you eat all your meals on time. You can't keep going on like this," I say as I hand her the cup. I'm concerned she's not taking good care of herself as she does for everyone else.

"I'm well, Nila. You don't need to worry about me." She sips the water in her cup. "Enough about me. Are you ready for the games? Did your sisters like their dresses?"

"They did."

'What's wrong?"

"Nothing," I say as I rise. I haven't told her about the book or the training with Dalia. I haven't told my sisters, either. I don't want to cause unnecessary worry. "You rest. I'll be back in the evening. I needed to make sure you ate."

"May the stars always favour you, my Nila," she says as she squeezes my hand.

Now that Kaku is cared for, I walk towards the east wing to my mother's room, brushing against a group of drummers who are heading to the throne room to entertain Papo and his guests.

I pause outside the door as I hear the lock click.

"Don't be long," Mother's servant, Beru—a tall bald woman—urges as I walk inside.

Mother is sitting on her bed. She looks frail. Her collarbone is pronounced, and her hair has grown so thin, I can see her scalp.

"What is it?" she asks as she looks away. She never stares my sisters and me in the eye as she fears we might influence her womb to carry another girl. She rarely spends time with us, and we were all raised on goat milk because she refused to breastfeed us. One time when Nakai was a child, she almost died from a fever, and our mother never even stepped one foot in Kaku's room to see her.

"Are you attending the games tomorrow?" I ask, sitting on the bed beside her. The sun would do her good—her skin is dry like ash. She needs to get out of this room more often.

"The games do not concern me," she says as she rubs her belly absent-mindedly.

I nearly gag as Beru hands her a glass full of bull's urine mixed with Kaba's magic potions. She drinks it every morning and evening believing it will help her conceive a boy.

"You need to come. You need to get out of this room more often," I say as I take the empty cup from her hand and hand it back to Beru.

"Nila, it does not concern me. Besides, your Papo asked me not to attend, and whatever he says is right. We all have a role to play for Sheba, and mine is here in this room." She rubs her belly again and again and then lies down on the bed facing away from me.

"I'll see you soon," I say as I try to touch her hand.

She snatches it away from me as if I've scalded her with a hot flame. I walk out and lean against the door as tears roll down my face.

Chapter Six

"I heard that some people saw a shooting star last night," Nakai says as my sisters and I head to the fields for the games the next day.

"Really, when?" I ask as we walk down the last steps. I'd spent most of the night in the archives.

"At dawn."

"Oh." I look around the field. At that time, I'd gone back to my bed and was stuck in a nightmare where Beru was forcing me to drink bull's urine. I'd clenched my teeth and refused to open up. I woke up exhausted today.

"I say we split up. Walking together makes us look childish," Sahara declares.

She looks beautiful with a rainbow of beads in her freshly braided hair and a flowing dress reaching her feet. Now she's eighteen, she doesn't fancy walking in packs, especially with our younger sisters, and I know she wants to mingle with some of the princes and princesses her age.

"But someone needs to keep an eye on Makeda," I remind her.

I wish I could, but Papo has asked me to join him as he welcomes the envoys of royals into the fields. Dalia has dressed me in a blue silk dress that's snug around my waist and my hips as it flows to my feet. It is deceivingly modest, yet every curve of my body is under display. When I looked at myself in the mirror this morning, I didn't hate it—it's beautiful. My hair is not in a bun, the moisturized kinky curls unbound and falling on my shoulders.

"I agree," Sahara says as she turns to our sisters. "Nakai, you stay with her and watch after her."

"But...but Etana can watch her. I want to be alone, too," Nakai replies as she pouts.

"I've put you in charge. The three of you stick together, you understand?" Sahara commands.

If it were up to me, I wouldn't let my younger sisters attend the games, but Papo commanded everyone in the palace to attend.

"You just said that walking together is childish," Nakai counters.

I sneak away not wanting to be caught in the heated arguments that sometimes arise between my sisters.

"Well, I'm older than you, so you do what I say."

I can hear Sahara argue as I walk away. The citizens of Sheba are filing into the fields, excitement and anticipation in the air.

I arrive just in time as Papo welcomes Emperor Gedi of Bazina to the fields, together with his entourage. I stand beside King Mesati as part of the Sheba envoy.

"You are just in time. The Aksa envoy is here," King Mesati whispers as Papo talks to Emperor Gedi.

"Where?" I ask as I look behind the Bazina envoy.

"Grand Emperor Nefe, meet Emperor Teti and Empress Nakaaba of Aksa, the first empire, together with their son, Crown Prince Seni," Piayu, the royal announcer, declares.

I look past the tall emperor with a silver beard and the beautiful empress with locss that fall to hip length, and my cheeks heat up and my heart pounds as I look at the prince. He is simply the most gorgeous man I've ever seen. We lock eyes, and his full lips curve into a smile.

Striking upturned honey-coloured eyes dance with amusement. He has a sharp jaw, well-cut and precise. The sides of his hair are shaved, and the locss in the middle are tied back as they fall on his back. His dark skin is smooth and has a healthy glow.

"Welcome to Sheba. My name is Nila." I offer my best diplomatic smile as I extend my hand in greeting. His hand is firm and large, and I hope he doesn't notice how sweaty my palm is.

"Thank you, Princess Nila."

His voice is deep and crisp, and my stupid belly clenches when he says my name.

We stand next to each other as our parents talk. He's wearing purple just like the rest of their envoy. Although they don't wear any flashy adornments, I've never seen such a luxurious fabric before. It snags perfectly on his well-toned, muscular arms.

He stands with his back straight, chest out, legs in wide stance, eyes scanning the fields. At this angle, it's as if he is both behind and beside me as if to shield me, and his liquorice scent makes me want to stand even closer.

"I hear you want to fight the Kilishi today, Seni?" Papo asks, assessing him with a smile on his face.

"Yes, Grand Emperor," Seni says as he flashes perfect white teeth.

"Nila, why don't you show Seni around before the games begin?" Papo cocks his head at us.

"Yes, Papo," I say as I swallow. Why doesn't my voice sound like my own? It is too high-pitched. It's not the purr Dalia taught me. It's way worse than my actual voice. I forget a whole month of lessons by just being in his presence. "This way, Prince Seni."

Chapter Seven

I point towards the palace, and he trails behind. He catches up and walks beside me on my right.

"Why do you want to fight the Kilishi? Do you have a death wish?" I ask, feeling angry he is deliberately putting himself in such danger. "Do you even know what they are?"

With Aksa being so secluded from the rest of the highlands, maybe he didn't know what the creatures could do.

I notice my voice is rising, yet according to the lessons I've received from Dalia, I'm supposed to be calm, to talk less, and bat my eyelashes, but I'm so angry, I forget everything.

"I heard about the hybrid creatures yesterday. They should not be allowed to live. It is a great offense to nature," he says, using a sharp tone with me as if I'm the one who made them.

"So you are only fighting them for nature's sake?" I ask as I stop.

"Yes. Someone has to do it."

There he goes scolding me again.

Confessing his hate for the creatures and telling me he wants to fight for nature makes him even more attractive in my eyes. But still, it's a misguided quest, and he might die. I need him to understand that.

"In that case, then we should head this way, I want you to see them first. Maybe then, you'll change your mind and forfeit," I say, changing course of our path and heading south towards my grandfather's statue.

"I won't," he objects.

"This is Nefe the second," I say, pointing at my grandfather's statue. He has a long face and a tight smile. I never met him, but I've heard Papo is a better version of him, which says a lot because with how much I know about Papo, I cannot imagine him being a better version of someone.

I reach for the statue's hands and find the lever on his left thumb. The ground below opens to reveal stairs, and we walk downwards to the tunnels. The Kilishi are kept here in cages.

"They are not fed for three days in preparation for the games," I say as we take a corner.

There are flaming torches hung over our heads on the walls.

"They will be led out through this tunnel." I point at a path that goes directly to the fields where the games are happening. "We are almost there," I say as I cover my nose with my elbow.

I can smell their stench from here. It's like rotting flesh. I stop as I hear noises. Two people are arguing.

"This is the right chance. The emperor and all his royal friends are out there. We should release them, set them free, and let them do the work for us. We die of hunger in the provinces while he sits here in his palace, drinking and holding games. It would be justice to see him die by his creation," a male voice says.

"But there are women and children out there. I believe we should capture one and release it in the throne room later when he is alone," the second male voice replies.

It sounds familiar.

"Ssh." Seni places a finger over my lips and pulls me closer to him.

His hardened body feels like a brick wall against mine.

The men stop talking.

"Someone is here," the second male voice says.

I hear footsteps as they walk in our direction, and I move closer to Seni to make myself small.

From behind us, a third man approaches. He looks rough. He wears an eye patch, and half of his left ear is missing.

"Well, if it isn't the emperor's daughter and her friend," he says as he moves closer.

The other two men join in. I know one of them—he is Papo's wine bearer. He looks a little different now without his uniform.

"She has seen your face. She knows who you are," his friend says.

Seni stands in front of me to cover me and punches the man with the eye-patch in the face. He staggers backward. The second man closes in. Seni punches him in the gut, and he falls to his knees.

The eye-patch man approaches again. Seni locks the crook of his elbow around his neck until the man goes unconscious. I see the wine bearer run away. Seni starts towards him but I take his hand to stop him as I hear the locks open and the unmistakable snarl of Kilishi.

"Run," I say as I look back to see one of the ugly beasts stalking towards us.

Seni wants to stop and fight them off, but I grab his hand as we run back through the tunnel. But instead of finding ourselves at the fountain's entrance, I hear the voices of a multitude. Stars help me, I panicked and took the tunnel to the fields.

We run into the field and find ourselves surrounded by not one but three Kilishi. How different the day has turned out. For the last month, I'd been prepared to flirt and dance with serpentine grace for Seni. I did not expect I'd be in the fields surrounded by Kilishi with him.

I look up at the podium where Papo and the royal families are standing. Nasou speaks to him and points at three archers who are approaching the fields. Papo raises his hand, and the archers retreat, leaving us alone.

"Let the games begin," he announces as he sits down, then raises the chalice in his hand to Seni and me. I hate him.

Seni rips open his shirt and takes off two daggers strapped to his back, gives me one of them.

"Stay by my side no matter what," he says as one of the creatures leaps towards us.

Chapter Eight

Seni throws off the first Kilishi, and it falls away. The second one has its eyes on me, and he rolls on the ground with it. The crowd cheers. The first one is approaching again, and so is the third. I hold on to the dagger in my hand and crouch, ready to strike. When it gets too close, fear fills my heart. I close my eyes as I fall behind.

I open my eyes as Seni lands a kick on the third one. The second, which looks a bit smaller, bares its teeth at me. I can take this one. The first one with patches of black on its coat leaps back towards Seni, angrier than it was before. I peddle back as the second one approaches me. It pounces on me, and its slimy saliva falls on my neck. Its claws start sinking into my chest, and I pierce its jaw with the dagger. But instead of falling off, it looks infuriated.

Seni throws it off my body.

"Did it hurt you?" he asks as he helps me up.

"No," I say as I stand.

My skin is burning where its claws sank in. I can see Seni is bleeding from the ribs, as well. I look at the second creature. At least I got it. The first one is limping, but the third one looks more determined than ever.

The three of them surround us again. The third one has got its eyes on me.

"Aim for the eye," Seni says as he faces the other two. He picks up one and throws it on the other. I hear a whimper.

"What are you waiting for? Come on!" I challenge the third one which is slowly walking towards me. I take my eyes off it for a second when I see Seni break the neck of the second. The first snarls at him as it runs towards him at full speed.

The third one is already on me, its teeth on my foot. Excruciating pain fills me as it pulls me by the leg. I'm going to kill it. I look at the podium where Papo is watching me, drinking wine from his chalice.

"Nila," Seni calls as he fights off the first creature. I hear as its neck breaks.

He starts towards me. The beast is now between us. I hear a whooshing sound in the sky, then I see a flaming stone fall on the Kilishi. A hole burns through its body, and it falls dead.

I look at Seni and then at the sizzling hot stone in the Kilishi's gut. Its look is of equal shock as it looks at me. The whole crowd has gone quiet.

"He is a Star Summoner," I hear someone shout. "The prince of Aksa is a Star Summoner!"

Seni kneels beside me and takes a look at the blood dripping from my foot.

"You need to see a healer," he says as he helps me up. I stand on one leg.

"You are bleeding, too," I say as I look at his bleeding ribs. There are claw marks on them. Blood is dripping down on the ridges of his toned abdomen.

My dress is shredded, the silk material torn at my leg and chest, and probably other places I can't see, too, because right now, all I can feel is the pain in my leg. My vision of the cheering crowd starts to fade.

"Nila," Seni calls me, holding my face between his hands.

I feel so tired, like I've used all my energy on that field, yet I didn't fight the Kilishi as much as Seni did.

"Tired," I whisper as I pass out in his arms.

Chapter Nine

I wake up in a sweat, looking at my surroundings. The shelves of ointments and the drying herbs hung on the roof let me know I'm at the healers' station. It is dark, and a lamp lights the room.

"You are awake," Seni says.

I look to my left and see him lying on a similar bed to mine. His ribs have been dressed up, and so have his knuckles. My chest and my leg are also bound up. The pain in my leg is considerably less than it was when I was in the field.

A bald man wearing white robes walks in.

"This is my cousin, Shebiku, our physician in Aksa. He is the one who has been caring for us." Seni says as he sits up.

"You were very brave out there, Princess," Shebiku says as he smiles at me. He places the back of his hand on my forehead.

"Thank you." I say, looking at Seni. "But if it wasn't for Prince Seni, I wouldn't be here, alive."

Shebiku scoffs as he looks at Seni. "You could have been faster, cousin. If you went for the jugular on its neck with the dagger, it could have been over before it started, and the princess would not have been hurt."

"Glad to know how much you care for me, cousin," Seni says as he rolls his shoulders.

"How do you feel?" Shebiku asks me, a concerned look in his eyes.

"I feel better. Thank you." I smile to assure him.

"I will place you under observation here for the rest of the night. I will be coming by every two hours to look at your wounds. These are creatures made with dark magic. We have to be careful we don't overlook anything."

"What about me? I'm hurt, too," Seni asks as he lifts his brow.

"You stay here and look after Princess Nila," Shebiku says as he pushes Seni back on the bed.

I do not fail to notice how careful he is as he does it, and the concern in his eyes for his cousin. He opens the door and leaves. Seni lies back on the bed.

"So you are a Star Summoner," I say as I turn on my side to face him. He doesn't answer but stares back at me with curious eyes.

"I'm so sorry you got hurt. I should have been faster. An Aksan warrior should not let the enemy draw even a drop of blood of an innocent."

"Don't be hard on yourself. The Kilishi are creatures of dark magic. I've never seen anyone face them and leave, but we lived, because of you," I say as I smile at him.

The door opens, and his mother, Empress Nakaaba, walks in followed by his father, Emperor Teti.

"Seni, how are you feeling?" she asks as she hugs him. He winces.

"I'm fine," he says, touching the bindings on his ribs.

His father pats him on the shoulder. "You did well, but you could have been faster."

"I know, Father."

"I love you, son." His father hugs him, and his mother joins in the three-way hug.

I sit up on my bed as I look at the bond they have. I wish I could have that with my parents, but I doubt any of them cares if I lived or not. I swallow.

"And you, Princess Nila." Empress Nakaaba faces me. "You were exceptional."

The three of them face me, and I sit up on the bed. She comes over and hugs me. Her locss have the sweet smell of coconut milk.

"You are special, Nila." The emperor touches my cheek with his thumb.

"Thank you." I'm touched they care. I rarely get affection, and when I find it, I bask in it.

"Shebiku will take care of you. By tomorrow, you will be almost healed," Empress Nakaaba says as she looks at my bandaged leg. "Take some rest, both of you. We will see you tomorrow."

She kisses me on the cheeks before they walk out.

"You have amazing parents, Seni," I say as I feel the bandage on my chest.

"Yes, they are. But they can be overbearing sometimes," he says, flexing his knuckles.

How I wish I was so loved by mine that I could call them overbearing.

The door opens again, and Kaku and my sisters walk in.

Makeda rushes in and hugs me. "Nila, you fought the Kilishi."

Her tone is filled with pride, and I forget the pain in my chest as she crushes into me.

"Careful, Makeda. Your sister is hurt," Kaku says as she takes my hand. "How are you feeling, Nila? I was here when they brought you in. Shebiku is a good physician. He is taking good care of you."

"I'm fine," I say with a smile.

My sisters crowd around me, hugging me, touching my face, and kissing my cheeks, and I realize I, too, am blessed with overbearing love in my life.

Chapter Ten

"Introduce us to Prince Seni," Etana whispers in my ear. Nakai and Makeda nod and giggle.

"Seni, these are my four wonderful sisters."

He sits up and flashes a gorgeous smile at them, My cheeks heat up.

"Sahara is the second born." Sahara waves. "Nakai is the third," I say as Nakai covers her mouth and giggles. "This is Etana. She follows Nakai." Etana hides her face behind Sahara's back. "Makeda is the last born." Makeda grins and waves.

"And this is Kaku." I squeeze her hand in mine. "She is like our second mother. She has loved us and taken care of all of us since we were born."

Kaku's eyes crinkle at the corners as she smiles. She squeezes my hand. "It's nice to meet you, Seni, and thank you for protecting Nila in the field. I can never thank you enough."

"It's my duty." Seni smiles at her. "It's an honour to meet you Kaku, Sahara, Nakai, Etana, and Makeda." He turns to each of them as he addresses them.

Etana whispers something to Nakai who squares her shoulders. "Etana is asking if she can touch your locss."

"Etana!" I snap at her, at the same time as Kaku and Sahara.

"It's fine," Seni says. "Yes, she can."

He unbinds his locss, and they fall on his face. He runs his hand through them sweep them back, except for one. I wonder how it would feel like to tuck it behind his ear.

Etana steps forward and takes the one lock in his hand.

"They are so soft," she says.

Nakai and Makeda join in as they touch Seni's hair. I'm embarrassed on their behalf—I've already told them many times it's improper to touch someone's hair like this, but then again, he has given his permission.

"Is it true you can summon a star?" Makeda asks as she gets on the bed and sits beside him.

Seni looks at me and then back at her. "I guess so."

"Did you come from Aksa on your horse?" she continues, again twirling a locs in her fingers, a little too roughly. She loves horses.

"Yes. His name is Eku. He is a black stallion. He is very fast, and he loves apples."

"Can we see him tomorrow?"

"Yes."

Etana whispers something to Nakai again, and I narrow my eyes at them. I hope it's not another inappropriate request.

"Are you married? Did you come with your wife?"

Valid question. I look at him, also wanting to know.

"No," he says, looking at me.

"But is there a girl you like?" Nakai asks as she reaches for the band in his hand and ties his locss back together at the top of his head.

"Yes, but I don't know if she likes me." He sighs.

I bet she is a tall Aksan beauty with locss that fall down her back, and she can fight a Kilishi better than I did. I don't know her, but I don't like her already.

"Why?" Nakai asks.

"Girls, it's time for us to leave so Seni and Nila can rest," Kaku announces. "It's also time for you to sleep," she says, helping Makeda off Seni's bed. My sisters protest, but Kaku manages to get them out of the room. Sahara stays behind.

"I'll see you tomorrow." She hugs me and leaves.

"My sisters can be a bit overbearing," I say as I lie back on the bed. The pain in my leg is back, and I hope the two hours are almost up so Shebiku can come back again.

"They are perfect. I wish I had siblings," he says as he loosens the band on his locss.

"You are an only child, then?"

"Yes. But my father has ten brothers, so I grew up with a lot of cousins, but I've always wondered if having a sibling would have felt different." He rests his head on the crook of his bulging arm as he faces me. "How was it for you growing up?"

"Great," I say, remembering my childhood. "First, it was Sahara and me, then Nakai, Etana, and Makeda. I'm the oldest, so I had to make sure they were alright, and I had to break up fights and care for scraped knees." I pause, lost in a memory. "We had this elephant, her name was Hawi, and during the sunny season, we'd line up at her watering hole, and she'd splash us with water. She also allowed us to ride on her back. I had to make sure everyone got equal time. She was quite a sport, and she was so smart, and she followed us everywhere around the palace. The servants would complain because her dung filled the hallway. She'd be our lookout as we stole bread from the kitchens. I think the kitchen staff loved her, too, because she was the worst lookout because of her size—anyone could see her standing by the door. But she'd trumpet when the kitchen was empty, and we'd rush in for the fresh, hot bread."

"Sounds like you had a great childhood. Is Hawi still alive?" Seni asks.

"No, she died," I say, staring at the drying herbs tied in bunches on the ceiling. Some are still green, others completely dried up.

I still remember the night Hawi died. I was in my room when I heard her trumpet three times. This was her distress call, like when it rained because she was afraid of thunder, and I'd go and stay with her in her shed.

This particular night, I heard her trumpet, but there was no rain or thunder, so I got out of bed and followed her cries. I found her tied up behind the spice barns. Five guards were holding onto the ropes on her feet, and Kaba, the wizard, had a blade carving out her ivory. I ran towards him and tackled him, but two guards pulled me back.

"You can't do this," I yelled as they dragged me away. I kicked the air as hard as I could trying to free myself.

"Stop this," I demanded. Hawi tried to stand up to help me, but she was held down, and I could see blood dripping down her trunk as Kaba pulled out the ivory. She died looking at me, and I sank to my knees and bawled my eyes out. My heart felt as heavy as a rock.

The next day, they'd taken away her body.

"Where is Hawi?" Etana had asked me. My sisters were worried as they stood outside Hawi's empty barn.

"She went back to the forest," I'd said. "She will be happier in the forest with the rest of the elephants, and she will have a lot of space to run around anyway," I told them. I had cried all night in Kaku's room as she held me in her arms.

"I will miss her," Nakai had said. "I can't believe she left without saying an elephant farewell."

I look over at Sahara. I could tell she did not believe a word I'd just said. There was a lump in my throat, and my lips were trembling as I tried to answer Nakai. "I think—" I stopped speaking as tears welled up in my eyes.

Sahara had intercepted. "I think she knew we would understand because friends understand."

Nakai, Etana, and Makeda were sad, but they walked away towards the watering hole where we'd spend most of our time with Hawi.

Sahara had stayed behind with me.

"I know she is dead. I saw guards carrying lots of meat towards the kitchens, so I asked them where they got it," she'd said as she wiped tears from her eyes with the back of her hands.

"Kaba killed her and took the ivory," I'd said as I lowered my head. The bright sun hurt my sore eyes from crying all night.

"Don't eat the meat today. I heard the kitchen staff say that a frog jumped into the stew," I warned my sisters as we walked back to the palace.

Chapter Eleven

"Is everything well? You have been very silent," Seni asks as he comes to sit by my bed.

His smile drags me back to the present, in the healers' station.

"I'm well." I sit next to him, and my arm rubs against his.

"Shebiku will be here soon," he encourages. He takes the linen sheet from his bed and puts it around my shoulders.

I bite my lip as my leg throbs with pain. He pulls me close, and I place my head on his shoulder without thinking. It feels easy to do it.

"Tell me something about Aksa," I say, staring at the door, praying Shebiku will walk in any minute.

"Aksa is more about her people. We value the family unit, and we take care of each other." His voice distracts me from the pain.

Shebiku walks in, and I sigh. He looks at me and rushes forward.

"You couldn't tell she was in pain?" he asks Seni as he unbinds my leg.

The bite marks of the Kilishi have turned green. I'm shivering from cold, but at the same time, I'm sweating. He looks around the ceiling, reaches for a bunch of herbs, throws them in a mortar, and grinds furiously. Seni helps me lie back on the bed.

Then he reaches for a jar with white powder and mixes it in the pestle before adding water.

"Drink this," Shebiku says.

Seni takes the cup from his hands and places it on my lips. It smells terrible, and I gag. Slowly, I take a few sips and start feeling sleepy. Shebiku starts washing my wound.

"Am I going to lose my leg?" I ask as I battle to keep my eyes open.

"No, you are not. Don't worry yourself. You just lie back."

Seni smiles at me, and I close my eyes.

"It's her blood. It's poisoned. Quick, I need the serum." I hear Shebiku's voice echo in my ears as I drift off to sleep.

I wake up the next morning, and the first thing I look for is my leg. It's still intact and attached to my body. I sigh with relief. Seni is lying on a chair next to my bed. One of his locks has fallen over his left brow, down the side of his face to his neck. I lie back on my bed before I'm tempted to tuck it behind his ear.

My leg feels fine, more than fine—there is no pain at all, and I wiggle it. It feels great. I feel great and refreshed. I haven't slept like this for a long time.

I take another look at Seni. He is a good person, and so are all the other Aksans I've met. His parents are wonderful, and I probably still have my leg because of his cousin Shebiku. He said Aksans value family, they take care of each other, and they love each other.

I'm supposed to find a book that exposes the secrets of these people. I agreed to it before I met them, but now that I know how they are, I realise they are good people, and they have their reasons for keeping away from the rest of the highlands.

I have to forfeit my quest. I don't know what Papo will do to me. He'll marry me off to Eshi, and what about my sisters? I'll have doomed them to worser fates. My head hurts.

Seni opens his eyes and smiles at me, and I stare at him, my mouth wide open like a fool. He's gorgeous.

"How is your leg?" he asks as he stands up, heading towards me. His morning voice is low and gruff. I lick my lips, feeling parched.

"I feel like I'm all healed." I wiggle my foot.

"I'm sure you are. Let me get Shebiku so he can take a look at you." He winks at me.

He heads out and comes back with his cousin who carries a hot cup of milk and fresh bread in his hand.

"The tea in Sheba is nothing like I've ever tasted before," Shebiku says as he puts his morning meal down on the table.

"It's not tea. It's made from berries," I explain.

"Tea made from berries?" he asks as he unbinds my wound.

"Yes. The berries were recently found by one of the shepherds in the provinces. He realised that when his goats ate the berries, they'd get excited, so he chewed on some of the berries, and he says he felt alive. He plucked some and took them home to his wife. He refuses to say how the berries ended up in the milk, but when they drank it, they loved it. They shared it with their neighbours, who loved it, too." I pause for a few seconds. "Soon, people were coming up with suggestions on how to use the berries. Some dried them, and some roasted them. As time went by, people preferred to use it while roasted. People love it. We call it kafa."

I'm babbling because I'm nervous to see what my leg looks like. I'm sure the scars will be ugly. Not for vanity's sake, but I'd be crushed to carry a mark reminding me of the Kilishi on my body.

"Kafa. I love it. You should try it, Seni," he says as he points at his cup.

Seni shakes his head and declines, his eyes on my leg.

"There we go," Shebiku says as he pulls the last of the bindings away.

I gasp as I look at my leg. "There is no mark."

"Do you feel any pain?" Shebiku asks as I stand up. He presses on various points around where the bites are.

"No." I look at my leg, turning it side to side. There is only a little faded line, and I'm not even sure if it was there before or not. "Thank you," I tell Shebiku. 'I don't know how I can ever repay you."

"I'm glad to have helped you, Princess." He stands up. "Now let me go get more of the kafa."

When he leaves, I put on my sandals, and Seni and I walk outside. I need to go to my room and take off this tattered silk dress. When Dalia helped me put it on, it was meant to captivate, to mesmerise as I danced, but I'd been bitten in it, I'd bled on it, and soaked it in sweat.

The servants walk all over the courtyards to serve the royals of the highlands who are staying in the guest quarters.

"I need to go to my room and change. I'll meet you after," I say to Seni as we pass the Great Hall.

"Let me walk you," he offers, and we walk up to my room. "I've been thinking about what you said, that people can't figure out why the shepherd's wife put the berries in the milk the first time. It's a simple answer, isn't it?" He grins.

"Why do you think she did it? Why put it in the milk, of all places, why not in the food, what was she thinking? Maybe it was an accident."

"No, it wasn't an accident," Seni says as we get to my door.

"What was it, then?" I ask as I lean against the door.

I've been trying to solve this riddle for a long time. I think about it during the most random times, like when I'm packing spice in the barns, when I'm staring at the stars at night, or when I'm taking a bath like I'm about to.

"You get changed first. I'll tell you after you are done. Meet me at the fountain." He winks and walks away

I smile as I look at his back until he disappears down the steps.

Chapter Twelve

I usually take my time when taking a bath. Not Dalia's mandatory baths, but the ones I've drawn up for myself. I can spend hours in the water, but now, I clean up as fast as I can so I can go back and meet Seni.

I look at myself in the mirror, and the claw marks on my chest are completely gone, too. I wear a free-flowing yellow linen dress I usually wear to the spice barns. I comb out my curls and use a sash to tie my thick hair at my nape.

"The grand emperor wants to see you in the throne room, now." Nasou intercepts my path to the fountain.

I've been summoned again—this can't mean anything good.

"Nila, can you identify the man who opened the cages of the Kilishi?" Papo asks.

He doesn't even ask how I'm fairing or if I'm hurt. I'd been in the field surrounded by three

Kilishi, and he'd asked his archers to step down. He doesn't care if I live or die.

"It was dark, and I was scared," I say, looking at the door. I need to get to the fountain.

"I've been informed by Kaba that there are rebels in the palace planning an uprising to overthrow me. Some suspects have been arrested. Nasou will take you to the dungeon cells so you can identify the traitors."

I grudgingly follow Nasou as he takes the path past the archives to where Papo's infamous torture dungeon cells are. We go underground to the dimly lit tunnels. I can't believe this is another day finding me in the dungeons. Unlike the Kilishi dungeons that smell of rotten matter, these smell of fear, sweat, and faeces. If I'd taken a morning meal, I'd have vomited it all out.

We walk past cell by cell as I come face to face with the emaciated men, covered in grime all over their bodies. One reaches out a hand towards me, and there is another wailing as he faces the wall. The sound makes the hairs on my skin rise. This is not just a body crying, but a soul.

I recognize the man with the eye patch, but I walk past him. I don't see the wine bearer, but next to his cell, I recognize the second guy. The crescent moon tribal mark on his shoulder, I've seen it somewhere.

"I don't see anyone," I say as I turn to Nasou.

"Look again. The grand emperor said we shall not leave until you identify someone." Nasou coughs on the crook of his elbow. The stench in this place overwhelms him, too.

"You want me to condemn an innocent man to death?" I ask as we walk past the cell of the man with the patch. "I think we should leave. When you catch more people, let me know," I say as my stomach heaves and I dry retch.

Nasou nods and we walk out of the cell. When we are outside, he holds his knees and exhales before vomiting on his boots. I jump back as the brown liquid splashes on my feet.

"You owe me new sandals," I yell. I leave him there and go towards the kitchen.

"Neret, I need more bath water, please," I say and then run to my room before I run into Seni with all this stench on my skin.

After another scrub, I wear whatever I find first, which is a white silk dress, part of the clothes Dalia had made for me. None of her dresses are free-flowing. It clings to every part of my body, but it's comfortable. I head out and walk down towards the fountain.

When I make the last turn, what I see makes my heart drop.

Chapter Thirteen

The Aksa envoy is assembled there. They are leaving. I see Seni in a fresh pair of black pants and a shirt. He is talking to his parents and his cousin Shebiku who spots me first, and the others turn in my direction.

"Nila, we are leaving now. It was great to know you," his mother says as she kisses me on the cheeks before leaving for her carriage.

"Take care of yourself, Nila." His father squeezes my hand, then catches up with the empress and opens the door of the carriage for her.

"Kafa," Shebiku says as he salutes me and leaves. I laugh as I watch him go.

I'm left alone with Seni.

"I thought you were leaving tomorrow, or the day after?" I ask as I look up at him.

I don't want him to leave. My heart is heavy. Heavier than the night I watched Hawi die. Would I ever see him again? Would he come to the next

Nefe games? I'm sure by then, Papo will have married me off.

"Careful, I might think you enjoy my company." He smiles, staring at me intently.

"What if I do?" I ask, holding back the tears at the back of my eyes.

"Even if it's in a dungeon, or fighting hybrid creatures, or in a healer's station?" he asks as he takes my hand and places it on his chest.

"Yes," I whisper, not breaking eye contact. My palm is resting against his chest, and I can hear his heart beating, strong and steady.

He pulls me close, his hand tightening around my waist. I rest my head on his chest, burying my nose in his shirt. I inhale his liquorice scent.

"I'm going to miss you, Princess Nila."

"I'm going to miss you, too, Star Summoner," I say as I close my eyes. "You should stay a day longer. You owe me the answer to the shepherd's riddle."

He chuckles. "I'll tell you about it when we next meet?"

"Are you attending the games next year, then?" I ask, opening my eyes and looking up at him again. Even if Papo marries me off, I'll crawl back here if only to see him for one more day.

"I'm not sure about the games, but I'd like to invite you to Aksa. Would you like to come and visit my home?"

His hand rubs the small of my back. I feel my whole body heat up.

"I thought no outsiders were allowed."

"You are no outsider. You will come to Aksa as my esteemed guest." He tilts my chin up. "You have to come. Only then will I tell you the answer to this shepherd's riddle."

"If you will have me, then I'll be honoured to come." I smile and tuck the stray locs on his face behind his ear.

"You know when you say it in that sweet voice, it makes me think of another meaning."

"What? I said, If you'll have me, then I'll be honoured to come," I repeat the words. "Oh." I bite my lip.

"I'll be honoured when you come, Princess Nila," he whispers in my ear, then gives me an innocent kiss on the forehead.

I watch him as he gets on his black stallion and rides out of the palace gates.

When he is gone, I punch the air and giggle. The most gorgeous man I've ever met has invited me to his home in Aksa, the first empire. I'll get to see him again.

Chapter Fourteen

I make my way towards the archives to let Mari know that she can stop her research on Aksa. Knowing her, she'll have spent sleepless nights hauled in there, studying record after record.

"Mari?" I call as I open the door.

She is not at her usual station. I can hear voices behind the row of books. I walk towards the voice and find her binding the wounds of the wine bearer who was in the Kilishi dungeon with the other two.

I now remember where I saw the crescent moon tribal mark. It's on Mari's right shoulder.

"Nila, it's not what you think?" she says, rising.

The wine bearer stands up, too, his eyes watching me and the door.

"Don't tell me what I think." I pick up a book and hold it as a weapon between us. "I know what I'm seeing."

"Nila, calm down and think. He is not the enemy here. Look at him. Who does he remind you of?" Mari pushes the book away from my hands, and it falls with a thud. I'd never thought she could do something like that. Books are sacred objects to her. "Who does he look like, Nila?"

I look at the guard behind me, his long face and thin lips. His dark skin.

"Papo," I exhale.

I've walked past him so many times in the hallways and seen him inside the throne room—how could I have never seen it? He looks like Papo.

"Before you were born, sixteen years to be precise, the grand emperor toured Astabara with King Mesati, and he saw our mother. He asked that she be brought to him, and he had his way with her, even though she never consented. That's how Hemi was conceived," Mari says, picking up the book from the floor. "King Mesati found out about what had happened, and when he was born, he brought him here. The grand emperor refused to accept him as his child, but he allowed him to stay, as his wine bearer. Hemi is your brother, Nila, and he is mine." She dusts the book with her hands.

I look at the man behind her. I have a brother. Why did Papo reject him? I know he wishes my sisters and I were boys. Hasn't Mother been drinking bull's urine all these years so she can conceive a boy, or is there something else?

"That does not explain what happened, and I hear you are planning an uprising," I say as I look at the book in Mari's hands.

"He is the rightful heir to the throne of Sheba," Mira says, placing the book back on the shelf.

"That does not excuse what you and your friends were doing," I say, pointing a finger at Hemi. "You wanted to release those horrible creatures on innocent people. I almost died." I remember the pain in my leg, and how the bite marks had turned green.

"I'm sorry." His voice is soft. I've never heard him speak; I only see him in the throne room pouring wine for Papo. "The others thought it was the right thing to do."

"Are you ready to rule an empire if you cannot be in control of two people? If you cannot take responsibility for your actions?" I say, looking him up and down.

"I want him to feel the pain he's caused me throughout the years. I want to humiliate him the way he humiliates me when he flings his chalice at me. Do you see these scars on my forehead? These are cuts from his chalice. He calls me boy, he spits in my face. I've thought about poisoning his wine, but that would be too easy."

I take a step forward and hug him. "Welcome to the family, brother."

I understand him. I truly do.

"Don't let this place turn you into him. Go away from here, find your peace elsewhere. At least, you have a place to go to back in Astabara. I wish I did. I'd leave with my sisters and not look back." I turn to Mira. "Tell our brother he is on the wrong path. Tell him to leave the palace."

I say my piece and walk out the door.

I never thought I'd meet my brother like this. I walk towards Kaku's room. I can't wait to tell her about the good news, how Seni has invited me to Aksa. However, this new information about Hemi being my brother threatens to steal my joy.

But I'll not let anything steal my joy. I shrug it off and keep walking. I knock and open Kaku's door to immediately fall on her bed. She's the only person who keeps my secrets. The only person I tell what's going inside my head.

"He thinks his uprising will work." I scoff, then sniff my dress when I smell liquorice on me. Seni's scent is still there.

"Nila, I listen to people, those who live inside and outside the palace. It's true, an uprising is coming, if not from Hemi then someone else. The people are tired of the grand emperor's tyranny," Kaku says, folding a pile of clean clothes. "I've been thinking about our safety, about how to protect you and your sisters. I recently met an old friend. He came to see me while the games were going on. His name is Tesfaye. He was your father's chief astrologist. He was there the day you were born. He's started a sanctuary, a place where the grand emperor cannot find us. That's where the astrologers disappeared. Your sisters will be safe there, and so will you."

She then sits down on the bed beside me.

A place where Papo could never find us. I'd just wished this very thing a few moments ago when I spoke to Hemi. It'd be a dream come true.

"How do we talk to him when we are ready to leave?" This is too good.

"Leave that to me. I'll be meeting him every full moon from now on."

I notice the shy smile on her face.

"Every full moon?" I ask, feeling protective. "I need to meet this Tesfaye and see if he is right for you."

"We'd started talking before he left, but I couldn't leave with him. You were three days old, Nila," she says casually as she places the laundry inside a trunk.

"You stayed because of me?" I feel dizzy and guilty.

"Nila." Kaku closes her trunk and comes back on the bed. "Don't look at me like this. I chose you. I'd still chose you given the chance."

She hugs me, and my chin rests on her shoulder.

"But he is your true love," I whisper.

"No. I'm a mature woman, Nila. I'm not on a quest for blazing love. I need a companion. Someone to grow old with. I don't want to die without having lived that. If you want, I can arrange for you to meet him on the next full moon." She smoothes my hair with her hand.

"I won't be here on the next full moon. I'll be in Aksa. Seni has invited me to his home." I can feel my face light up as I say the words.

"He did?" Kaku asks as she cups my face. "Oh, my girl, I'm so happy for you. He is a good boy. When you were injured in the field and unconscious, I saw the way he carried you to the healers' room and cared for you. He wouldn't let Shebiku treat him until you were taken care of."

When I leave Kaku's room, I'm beaming, Seni cared for me when I was injured. I count down the days until when I'll see him again.

I find Kaba standing by the hallway, arms folded, frown on his face as always.

"Did you succeed on your mission?" he asks as he looks at my left leg where the Kilishi had bit me. His brows lift in surprise.

"How does it concern you, wizard? You want us to wear matching dresses, drink kafa as I tell you I've been up to?" I ask as I size him up.

He sighs. "Save your insults for someone who cares. I'm here to tell you that the grand emperor requests that you appear before him in the throne room, now."

My shoulders sag. I've been summoned, again, the second time today.

Kaba grins as he brushes past me. I lose my balance and almost fall.

Chapter Fifteen

"You are now in the presence of Grand Emperor Nefe of Sheba, the unconquered mighty stink," Piayu announces.

Stink? Did he say stink? I look forward to seeing if Papo has noticed, but he is too busy shaking his empty wine cup.

He hasn't noticed, just like he doesn't know that his wine bearer is not at work today because he is planning a rebellion to overthrow him. He is losing his mighty sting.

"Nila, get me the flask," he says, pointing at the wine flask a few feet from him.

I take it and refill his chalice.

"Did you get the invite to Aksa as we planned?" he asks as he gestures for me to refill his cup to the top.

"It didn't go as we planned," I say, tilting the flask to pour the wine." But I got invited to go to Aksa."

He empties his chalice for the second time. "Then we have to start preparations for your visit immediately."

"About the book." I square my shoulders. I know what I'm about to say will rile him up. I've forfeited our deal about the book. I cannot do this to Seni and his wonderful family.

"Forget the book. You are now the book. When you return from Aksa, I want you to tell me everything you see," he says as he huffs in my face.

I refill his chalice again, for the third time.

I spend the rest of the afternoon in the throne room as Papo's wine bearer. I've lost count of the number of times I've refilled his chalice.

In the evening, I walk slowly towards Dalia's quarters. I need to gloat that flirting and batting eyelashes didn't get me the invite to Aksa.

When I get to her room, her door is unlocked.

"Dalia?" I call as I enter.

My blood chills when I see her. Her left eye is so swollen, it doesn't close. Every part of her face is swollen. She sees me and tries to stand to wave me away, but she can't speak. She looks like she's battled ten Kilishi.

"What happened to you?" I ask, kneeling beside her.

There are marks on her wrists and ankles like she'd been tied up. She is trembling violently. The door opens, and Nasou walks in. His eyes dart to Dalia, and he kneels beside her and looks at her face.

Sorry, I couldn't come earlier. I had to wait until he was drunk," he apologizes, kissing her hand.

"Let me go find the healers," I say, standing at the door.

No. "Dalia shakes her head. "I'll be fine in a day or two. He'll be angry if he knows they were involved. He doesn't want anybody to know."

Nasou pours water from a blue flask on her table and uses a cloth to dab her lip which has been burst.

"This will help," he coaxes her as he dabs slowly. She hisses in pain and tries to push him away.

"Let me," I tell him, kneeling and picking up the cloth.

My hand trembles as I dab her eye and her cheeks. I'm the daughter of the man who did this. Is this why sometimes, she disappears and stays locked in her quarters? I thought she was out here dancing alone, drinking wine, and trying on silk dresses.

"Please, you have to let me help you. I can't leave you in this much pain. Let me come with Kaku. She's discreet, and she will help you. No one will ever know about it. You can trust her." I place the cloth back in the water and wring it out again. Her neck and collarbone are all bruised.

"I won't be long," I say as I head outside.

My head spins as I walk away. She is in so much pain. My blood boils as I walk past the throne room and hear Papo's bellowing laughter. How could he do this to her? From what she told me, this wasn't the first time. I'm tempted to walk in and confront him, but I know it would end badly for her.

"Poor girl," Kaku says as we head back to her room, her basket of herbs and potions in her hands.

The guards never scrutinize her as they know she deals with the pregnant women in the palace. When we enter back in, Nasou is speaking softly to Dalia, and she nods. He steps aside when he sees Kaku, but lingers close enough.

I look away as Kaku undresses her to examine the extent of her injuries. I fold my arms, stand by her window, and look outside. From here, you can see the horse racing fields.

"You have a broken rib, as well," Kaku says. I turn and see her rustle through her basket for ointment. "Drink this, it will help with the pain." She has a look of pity in her eyes.

"You can't bind the wounds. He'll know someone helped," Dalia says in a panicking voice.

"No need to worry. If he asks, then you tell him you did it yourself, with the help of the mirror," Kaku reassures her. "I'll come by again tomorrow."

"Thank you, Kaku," I say as she heads out.

"I have to go before my absence is noted," Nasou says to Dalia. "I'll see you as soon as I can." He kisses the back of her hands and stands.

"Find Neret. She is a kitchen maid. Tell her Princess Nila needs soup and bread, a warm flask of water, and another with milk," I say as Nasou walks past me.

"All right." He bends low so his giant frame can fit through the door.

When the food arrives, I feed Dalia spoonfuls of soup which she swallows with much difficulty.

"I miss home," she says as her glassy eyes stare into space.

"Tell me about your home," I ask as I dab the corners of her mouth. Talking will distract her from the pain, as it did for me after I was injured by the Kilishi.

"It's a small kingdom called Suwi, south of Sheba. I'm or was a princess." There's a dreamy tone in her voice. Kaku's sleeping potion is kicking in.

"I've always known you are a princess," I say as I urge her to take the last spoonful of the soup.

She smiles as she lies back on the bed. "We lived in peace and harmony, with my mother and father, sisters and brother, until the Grand Emperor came one day. Someone had told him he could find the book of Aksa there. He turned the place upside down and killed one of my brothers. My father was badly injured. He said he'd take me and let me go when they brought the book to him. We'd heard of Aksa, the first empire, but we didn't have the book he talked about." She then yawns into her palm.

"You need rest. Go on, sleep," I urge and cover her with the brown furs on her bed. I realize now why she was so interested in seeing me succeed in my quest for the book of Aksa. She hopes if Papo gets hold of the elusive book, he will set her free.

Mukami Ngari

Chapter Sixteen

The days slowly pass by, and after what feels like eternity, three weeks have passed, and I'm ready for my visit to Aksa. When I open my eyes in the morning, I'm surrounded by a sea of faces.

"Go away, all of you," I say as I get up. All my sisters are in my room. They are as excited about this visit as I am.

"Will you ask Seni if we can also come to Aksa next time?" Etana asks. When Seni was here, she couldn't look him in the face or speak.

"Who says there will be a next time?" I ask I strap my feet into sandals. I notice the sole of my right foot has a small patch of black, similar to how my left foot started. My left sole is now fully black.

I've been lucky to be invited to Aksa once. I don't want to think beyond that.

"We should give Nila time to prepare," Sahara says as she closes my trunk of clothes that I'll be carrying to Aksa. She'd been helping me pack.

One by one, my sisters hug me as they leave.

"You will be fine." Sahara hugs me.

She realizes I am nervous. I've been pacing around the room.

"I'm the first outsider to be invited to Aksa, Sahara," I say, biting my lip. I have to make sure that everything I do, every word I say is perfect. I have to represent the rest of the highlands well.

"Seni knew this when he invited you, didn't he? He chose to invite you. Don't let worry ruin your visit. Enjoy every minute of it."

There is a knock on the door, and Sahara goes to open. I follow behind.

Nasou stands awkwardly outside. In his hands are a pair of sandals that look small on his big hand.

"I had these made for you, Princess Nila," he says, handing me the sandals. In his hand, they look small, but in my hand, they are my size. I remember I'd told him he owed me sandals the day he vomited as we were leaving the dungeons.

"Thank you," I say, looking at the beautiful pair of sandals made with blue beads and brown straps.

He nods and walks away, his giant feet making the whole floor echo.

These past few weeks, I've discovered he's a gentle giant. I've seen him look after Dalia as she healed from Papo's assault.

"They are beautiful," Sahara says as she puts the sandals in my trunk. "Well, here is my gift, as well." She reaches for a small satchel I hadn't noticed placed on my table. She hands it to me, and I see it's a little carved elephant. "Let her be with you as you make wonderful memories, just like Hawi was with us when she was alive."

"It's the perfect gift." Tears well up in my eyes as I look at the carving.

Most of my wonderful childhood memories involve my sisters and me playing with Hawi, and Sahara knows it. By giving me this gift, she wants to assure me that my visit will go well. The anxious feeling in my stomach disappears. There is a knock on the door again, and we look at each other.

"You have so many visitors today," Sahara whispers, and we laugh.

I open the door, and I am shocked at who stands there.

"Mother?"

"Wait here," she tells Beru, her servant.

I close the door behind us. She's never been in my room before. I stand beside Sahara. We are shocked into silence as we look at her.

She looks around my room and then at us.

"Nila, I heard you are leaving for Aksa." Her fingers tremble, and she places them on her side. They are always on top of her belly as she rubs it. After Makeda was born, she's been with child six more times, but the children are not born alive.

"I came to wish you well," she says, looking around the room awkwardly. "Remember, we all must fulfil our duties for Sheba." She shakes her head as if it was meant to remain a thought in her mind. "When you were born, your father named you Nila, but I wanted to name you Kaya." She turns around and leaves.

How is that supposed to help me twenty years later after I'm born?

"You need to get ready. It's almost time to leave. I'll tell Neret to bring your bath water," Sahara says, squeezing me on the shoulder before she leaves.

Chapter Seventeen

Everyone at the palace is outside watching as I leave. I'll be traveling with a dozen armed soldiers for my protection. My sisters are standing next to Papo, and I look back and watch them wave as my carriage rides out of the palace gates.

The soldiers have been instructed to ride to the border of Bazina, near where the Aksa walls are, and then I'll be received from there. The rest of the entourage has to wait for me in Bazina until I come back.

When traveling through the highlands, I normally get tired by day two of riding. Now, we've been on the road for five days, and I feel fresh and invigorated. I'm holding the elephant carving in my hands as we enter Bazina. In a few hours, we will be at the borders of Aksa.

I look outside the carriage at the mountainous view of Bazina. I wonder if this same environment expands to Aksa. I take in a deep breath, enjoying the view.

"I can see the wall," the soldier leading the way shouts.

I peer closely, and from afar, I can see big bricks extending to the skies. We come to a halt as we are met by a barricade of archers clad in black from head to toe. They have scaled down from the high wall, and they have ropes tied to their waists. Their stern faces make my heart pound, and I squeeze the elephant carving in my hand.

"You will go no farther," one of them declares.

They part the way to reveal a black stallion riding towards us. I relax when I see the rider is Seni. I open my carriage and step out, putting the elephant carving inside the pocket of my blue cloak. I'm wearing blue, the official colours of Sheba, as I'm to walk into Aksa not only as myself but a diplomat of Sheba.

He gets off his horse and runs towards me. I run to him, too, and we meet in the middle, between Aksa's archers and Sheba's soldiers. He picks me up and twirls me around like I weigh nothing, and I yelp, feeling happy to my bones. He puts me down, and we hug. My awareness of him makes me forget everyone around us. I can feel his hands tighten around my waist. I can smell him all over me as my head leans on his toned chest. He smiles down on me, and I feel my body heat rise.

"I hope the ride here was not too hard on you," he says, caressing my chin with his thumb in a caring gesture.

I lean into his hand. "Not at all. I enjoyed the view all the way."

"I'm happy to see you, Princess." He takes my hand as we walk towards his horse. "Let me take you home."

I look back to see Sheba's soldiers handing over my trunk to the archers. Seni gets on his horse and helps me up.

"Don't worry. I'll bring you back safe and sound."

I wrap my hands tight around his waist, as we ride towards the walls.

The huge gates open, and we ride through to another gate, and when it opens, my eyes almost pop out of their sockets. I feel like I'm been living in a wasteland all my life.

"By the stars!"

The streets are not made of cobblestone but are paved with gold. There is a burst of colour everywhere with flower gardens along the sidewalk as far as my eyes can see.

"Welcome to Aksa," Seni says as he helps me down from his horse.

I gape as I look at the palace. It's carved from a single gigantic diamond, and it's on the side of a colossal mountain whose peak disappears into the blue sky.

"Am I dreaming, or is the palace carved out of a diamond?" I blink as the sun reflects a kaleidoscope of colours on the outer surface of the magnificent palace. This has to be the largest diamond I've ever seen.

"It is. That is Mount Kosai, where the palace is. It spirals up into five floors which house three hundred rooms. My father's courtyard is on the top floor, where he lives with my mother. His ten brothers—my uncles—live there with their families, as well." Seni laughs. "My courtyard is on the fourth floor, and my cousins who have joined the ranks of warriors live on that floor, too. The throne room is on the third floor, together with the Judges Hall as well as all commercial buildings. All official dealings of the empire happen here. On the second floor is where the courtyards of the twelve kings of Aksa and their royal families live. Then the soldiers occupy the first floor," Seni says casually.

He is used to all this glorious beauty. I wonder what he thought when he came to Sheba. It must have looked like a mud house to him.

"It is so beautiful." I take in a deep breath. I've never seen anything like it. There is no way that a place more beautiful like this exists, not even Nahu, the celestial city. "But not as beautiful as you," I chide Seni as we walk towards the palace.

He smiles and licks his lips.

"You grew up here?" I ask as we pass by a statue of a man with locss reaching to his feet. It is carved out of a diamond, too. "All my life."

It's too much to see all at once, and I stop walking. Weird-shaped birds are hovering in the sky. One of them descends and flies to where we stand. My knees feel weak as it stares straight at me. It is featherless, smooth as an egg, yet it's alive.

"These are our welcome drones," Seni says, as if I'm supposed to know what that means.

"Welcome. I'll now take your blood pressure and temperature," it says, and I stay frozen in place.

"What magic is this?" I whisper as the bird moves around me.

"It's not magic. It's technology." Seni taps his ear and speaks. "Shebiku, she is going into shock, I need your help."

Shebiku appears almost immediately, flying in on an oval object.

"Nila.' He peers into my eyes with a weird light. His voice sounds like an echo. He snaps his fingers. "Breathe," he shouts. "Pass me the water bottle," he says to Seni who opens a little flask.

I take the cold water. It tastes like the spring water from Astabara.

"She is fine, but she should rest first before you explain everything else."

"No, I'm well," I say on a deep breath. "Tell me now, what is this place?"

I turn to face Seni.

He swallows. "Time has always moved differently in Aksa than it does for the rest of the highlands. While we share the same environment, Sheba is in first Millennium BC, and Aksa is in the year 2149 AD, which means we are six thousand and twenty years ahead. Let's sit on the bench."

He points at one of the long chairs I see all over the flower garden. They are carved out of diamonds, too.

"Our ancestors lived in a world which had great technological advancements. They created innovative solutions to issues and made great strides in medicine, communication, artificial intelligence, and science among other fields. However, some of their creations caused harm to their surroundings and their people. The air was poisoned with smoke and lethal gases. Some weapons caused mass destruction, and a lot of people were killed in senseless wars.

"Their world was becoming inhabitable, and the elite were leaving in ships and sailing to the stars in search of new worlds. Those who were left behind lived underground to hide from the sun's fierce rays. Sehuti, our ancestor, together with other scientists across the continents, came together to find a way to help save the common people.

"They built inventions that would transport people to timelines free from pollution. People of all races, creeds, and colours went back to different timelines. But they made agreements they would not carry these weapons of destruction into these new worlds, so they left behind guns, bombs, and everything that caused high carbon emissions.

"That was in the year 2049, which is a hundred years ago. When our ancestors first arrived here at Mount Kosai, the empires of the highlands had not formed. They formed the first empire. At first, they mingled with the native people here and learned their languages. They taught them a few things. However, some of the people were hostile and plotted to annihilate the Aksan people. So to avoid war and to keep peace and order, Aksa created these walls to keep to themselves," Seni says as he gestures at the walls.

I take a deep breath, looking around. I'd expected I'd find something different here, like caves filled with gold and beautiful waterfalls, but not this. I now understand why Aksa keeps to themselves. The rest of the highlands would kill for this. Papo would do anything to get his hands on this. If he knew what's on the inside, he'd start marching here immediately for this magic called technology.

I stand up and start looking around, and Seni follows behind, giving me the space I need.

Two young girls who are running around the flower gardens wave at us.

Standing at the palace steps, his mother and father are waiting for us with beaming smiles. They are floating on square-shaped platforms, holding hands and wearing purple robes. His mother is wearing a diamond-encrusted flower in her hair, and his father is carrying a diamond-encrusted sceptre. The worth of that alone would feed a province in Sheba.

"Welcome to Aksa," Emperor Teti says as he shakes my hand firmly.

"Welcome." Empress Nakaaba kisses me on the cheeks.

"Your home is beautiful and different," I say.

"The rules exclusively say no outsiders, but I see you've made an exception for your son as always, Teti," a man with the ochre-coloured locss says and stares at me.

Mukami Ngari

Chapter Eighteen

"That's enough, Tehi," the emperor says as he dismisses the man, who sneers at me before floating away towards the flower gardens.

"Ignore my uncle. He is like that to everyone," Seni says as he rubs my arm.

He helps me up to the square platform, and I grab his arm with all my strength as it leaves the ground.

We float across the soldiers' floor, up to the second floor, and onto the top floor of his parents' courtyard. Luxurious red rugs cover all the surfaces, and everything looks clean and sparkly, not a speck of dust in sight.

We float towards what I assume is a banquet hall—I've never been anywhere like this. The table and the eight chairs around it are carved from the same diamond making the exterior of the palace. Everything else in here is. Whoever made the palace carved everything inside it either from top to bottom, and I wonder what type of tools could have done this.

I'm stunned by everything I see as we alight from the object. I stand and look around as the emperor and empress sit.

"I'm sorry," I say when I realize they are staring at me. "I've never...it's...everything is a marvel."

Seni points to the chair beside him, and I sit down. There are trays of fruits. I see bread and lamb, but I don't recognize the food in the rest of the bowls. It smells delicious, and my mouth waters. I haven't eaten since morning. I watch as the emperor serves the empress food from the various bowls and hands it to her. She feeds him lamb from the plate, and he dips bread into the stew and feeds her.

I serve myself some of the food, and so does Seni, and we eat in silence. The sweet flavour of the stew explodes in my mouth. I wash it down with the wine in my chalice. Here, a chalice is common—back home, it's only reserved for Papo and his kings. Beside me, Seni is watching as I eat as if it's the most fascinating thing he's ever seen.

"I think watching you eat is now my favourite thing to do," he whispers to me.

I feel a burning in my cheeks as I look over at his parents, afraid they heard what he said. But they are too engrossed in helping each other eat and drink.

After we are done with the meal, Seni takes me down to the fourth floor, where his courtyard is. As we walk in, I see a wall of weapons—daggers, blades, arrows, and hammers in the common room. I can hear voices in some of the rooms as we pass by, and I remember that he said some of his cousins lived with him on this floor.

"Welcome to my home."

He smiles as he opens the door and shows me into an expansive room. There is a mahogany chair that could fit five people, covered in black furs. I hear the sound of music but cannot tell where it is coming from. He claps his hands, and the room becomes brighter. Not everything here is carved out of a diamond, like in his parents' room. The chair faces outside, from where I can see the mountain. I would enjoy waking up to this view every morning.

There is an imposing table with a bowl of various fruits placed on the table. Everything here is in its place. There are two chairs in the corner next to a row of books. We walk through the hallway where we pass a room with a modest-sized bed with white furs on it, then we pass three other similar rooms. Each room has a bathing area, and the tubs inside are carved from the diamond that built the palace. I realise how tired I am, looking at it. Seni stops at the end of the hallway.

"And this is my bedroom," he says as he leads me inside, his hand on the small of my back.

Inside is a bed covered in black furs like the ones on the seat. It is enough to fit five of me, and I wonder how it would feel to roll on it.

In the corner is a table and two chairs carved from the diamond. Part of his bedroom wall is covered with weapons, too. I see blades and daggers of all shapes and build. There is a room with built-in shelves where his boots are stored on one side and his robes on the other. His bathing area has a washing sink and a big tub. He opens the door to the outside.

"Last is the pool on the balcony," he says about the beautiful, clear body of water. From here, the mountain looks even closer.

"All of it is beautiful," I say, wishing I could dip my toes in the water.

"You must be tired. I will show you the rest of the palace later."

We head back inside, and I sit on the comfortable chair and swing my legs.

"I'm not tired," I say as I yawn. I am tired, but I want to see as much of Aksa as I can. I've seen and heard things I never thought were possible, and I want to see more.

"So when we were in the field fighting the Kilishi, did you use the technology magic to make the star fall from the sky?" I can hear the music inside the room, but I cannot see the person singing. It is a beautiful, strange melody that makes me relax.

"No, that was a meteor. Our scientists are still trying to figure out why there have been so many meteors falling in Sheba. That's why we accepted the invite to the games. If there is a meteor storm coming, we need to prepare, and warn the rest of the highlands."

He sits in front me and rolls up the sleeves of his shirt.

"Why did you invite me to Aksa? I'm the first outsider to be invited. Why?" I ask and bite my lips nervously, waiting for his answer.

"Because when I first saw you, I knew you were mine."

He places his thumb on my chin, and my lips part. He leans in for a kiss, and I close my eyes. I hear a strange sound coming from his pockets, and I open my eyes.

"What?" he asks as he touches his ear. "I'll be right there." He sighs as he stands up. "I'm needed on the second floor. I'll be back as soon as I can, and then, we can continue where we left."

"Is everything well?" I ask as he helps me stand up.

"A man has committed one of the worst crimes in Aksa. He was found with the materials used to make a forbidden weapon called a gun." Seni smiles. "You take a little rest, freshen up, and when I return, I'll take you to your welcome ceremony," he says as he leads me to one of the rooms adjacent to his. "I'll be back for you in three hours."

"Ceremony?" I ask, panicking. I didn't expect there would be a ceremony and I'd be the guest.

"Yes, we have all been waiting for you, Princess. Me more than others."

He winks as he closes the door behind me.

Chapter Nineteen

When Seni comes back three hours later, I'm nervously waiting by the door.

"How many people are there going to be?" I ask as I fidget with my fingers.

I've never had a celebration held in my honour before, and I'm not sure what is expected of me. Do I have to speak to all of them?

"It doesn't matter. All you have to do is smile and shake hands, and I'll do the introductions," he says, walking towards his room. "I'll change clothes, and then we'll leave."

I sit down on the fur-covered chair and wait. A few moments later, Seni emerges wearing white pants and a matching shirt.

I'm wearing a white and gold dress, which fits me perfectly like it was made for me. The material clings to my body. The sleeves of the dress are gold, and the vines swirl down to the bottom. I found the dress placed in my room, as my trunks had not arrived yet.

Seni is wearing a diamond-encrusted necklace of a ram. His locss fall behind his back. He looks gorgeous, and a whiff of his liquorice scent which I'm getting used to makes my belly clench.

"You look beautiful, delicious." His eyes roam up and down my body. "I have a gift for you."

He is holding a small pouch, and he opens it to reveal a diamond-encrusted necklace with the symbol of a bow and arrow. He helps put it around my neck.

"It's perfect," I say, fondling it in my hands. "Thank you."

I tuck my hand under the crook of his arm, and we float on the platform out to the flower gardens.

"What happened to the man with the forbidden weapon?" I wave back at an old lady with an orange dress and matching scarf.

"He was dropped in the crater. The wings of justice drone, which are the drones used in the Judges' hall, carried him over to the open crater past Mount Kosai and dropped him there."

Seni picks a sweet-smelling red flower and hands it to me.

When we arrive at the ceremony, on the green grounds away from the flower gardens, there is a group of people gathered around a fire. They are laughing and dancing in each other's company. Seni introduces me as we get off the platform and it flies away. Some of them look happy to see me, and I also see others eye me with suspicion. I stay close to Seni, and when we are separated because

I'm speaking to someone, I can still feel his eyes on me at all times.

When we go back to his home, it is late at night. The bath water here flows into the tub, and I enjoy a long soak in it before going to bed. When I sleep, I dream of hovering objects and falling stars.

The next two days pass by quickly. From morning to evening, I spend the whole day with Seni touring around Aksa. I ask endless questions, and he answers them patiently.

He'd taken me to give Shebiku a jar of kafa I'd carried for him. He was overjoyed, and I learned they called it coffee, and he'd never tasted anything as pure as the one in Sheba. It had almost tasted entirely different from what he was used to.

Later, Seni walks me down to the third floor so he can show me what a mall is.

When we are back in his home, I realise they have no servants here in Aksa, but everything works efficiently. Their magic technology helps them make their food and clean their house. I sit on the chair, fascinated as a circular object whirls around his room cleaning it.

I feel sad because tomorrow is my last day here, and then I'll go back to Sheba, and back under Papo's thumb.

On the last day, I'm sitting by the pool of water in Seni's home looking at the mountain before me and its peak that touches the cloud.

"The weather is perfect for a swim," he says as he takes off his shirt and jumps in the water, his top half bare.

He splashes water on me, and I scream. I take off my dress and get in the water in my undergarments. I swim past him, and he chases me. After a thrilling chase, he catches up with me and hugs me from behind.

I turn around, and he kisses me. His hand is at the nape of my neck, and my soft body entangles with his hard masculine one. It's fast and urgent like we've been starving for each other our whole lives. When his thumb brushes against my nipple, I feel a tremor that runs through my whole body, and I fist his locss in my hands as my legs shake.

I feel like if we weren't in the water, I'd have already combusted into flames. My whole body is on fire, and I want more of him.

"Seni," I beg.

"I take birth control, the men in our time do," he says.

"I do, too. I drink a portion."

He positions my legs on his hips, and he holds me by the waist as his thick sex struggles to enter my warm core. I moan, burying my face in the crook of his neck as he sits all of his incredible length inside me.

He moves in and out as my sex clenches around him, the sound of my cries and his grunting echoing all around us.

I come and collapse against his chest, and he curses as he empties inside me.

When we get out of the water, we dry ourselves up and lie down on his bed.

Tomorrow, I'll be on my way back to Sheba, I think as I run my fingers down the ridges of Seni's abdomen. My limbs are entangled with his, and I listen to the beating of his heart.

"Don't leave. Stay here in Aksa with me," he says before he kisses my lips.

"I wish I could, but I can't. My sisters need me."

"They can come live with us," he says as he flips me on top of him. "There is enough room for them."

"I don't want to cause you any trouble," I say as I straddle him.

I'd rather use these last few hours making memories. I slide down his thick sex and pause to get used to his fullness. Then I start moving up and down as I control the pace, my eyes never leaving his. I can feel the rapid beating of his heart against my palms.

He flips me over and is now on top of me. I lock my legs around his waist and meet him halfway as he moves. My hands are on top of my head, clasped with his. I arch my back as he bottoms out. It feels like my heart will burst as we both come.

Chapter Twenty

"I want to see you again, soon," Seni says as we ride out the gates and into Bazina, back in the highlands. The contrast to Aksa is glaring.

"So do I."

We pass by his archers, and he stops. He takes my hand and helps me down from his stallion. I can see Sheba's soldiers waiting for me. With my new set of eyes, everything looks gloomy and the colours seem dull.

"Can I see you next month?" Seni asks, tilting my chin and peering into my eyes.

"Yes," I say, closing my eyes as he kisses me, slow and long, holding me tight against his body.

I wave as I walk back to the carriage, and we start riding back home, to Sheba. I look back and see him still standing there. I lose sight of him when we take a curve in the road. Tears fall down my cheeks, and I wipe them away. The road is long and bumpy. The journey feels endless.

As we near the palace, I see my sisters running towards me, and the heavy feeling in my heart ebbs away as I run to kiss them.

"How is Aksa?" Makeda asks.

"Oh, they have many horses. You would love it," I say, patting her back. They follow me up to my room as Sahara carries my trunk.

"Sheba's palace is bigger, but the people there are very happy, and they have ceremonies. They sing and dance." I smile remembering something else entirely different—Seni and me in his pool of water. "Aksa is about its people."

I've decided that's the story I will stick to, especially when Papo summons me to his throne room, which I know he will do soon.

When I'm left alone at night, I cannot sleep. I reach deep inside my pockets and take out the archer necklace I'd taken off before we entered the gates of Sheba. I look at it in the gleaming moonlight. I will see Seni again in a month, and I'm counting down the days.

The next day, I'm woken up by a loud bang on the door. I get up and readjust to my surroundings. Nasou is standing by the door, and I know what he wants to say: I've been summoned.

"Tell him I'll be there soon," I say as I close the door and lean against it. Papo is not an easy man to lie to, and I hope my voice will not betray me. But I can do it, and I will, for Seni and Aksa.

"Sheba is bigger. Aksa is about its people," I recite as I walk down the hallway.

When I walk into the throne room, however, I'm not only met by Papo, but I see Kaba, and next to him, I see Prince Eshi of Kush. Next to him is a man with pitch black eyes and a white, glowing line along his chin, wearing a long black cloak.

"Nila, we are all very excited to hear about your visit to Aksa," Papo says as Hemi refills his wine chalice. He came back, the fool.

"Aksa is beautiful, the people are friendly. Most of them are humble farmers. But I'd say Sheba is bigger and better." I say, staring into his eyes.

"I've wanted to see it for so long, you are now the book I've been looking for. Would you open up your mind to the mage, so he can show it to me?"

"As you wish, Papo," I say, looking at the pitch-black eyes of the mage.

As the mage places his hands on my temples, I think of the walls of Aksa, the long walls that reach up to the skies.

"Open!"

I hear a rumbling voice in my head, but the mage does not move his lips.

The wall is tall, and it reaches to the skies, and there is mist all around. He lets go of me and looks at Papo.

"Nila, you are not hiding anything from us, are you? That would be cruel of you," Prince Eshi says, baring his teeth which are too big for his mouth.

"You deny me Aksa, after everything I've done for you?" Papo asks as he steps forward.

"Aksa is a humble empire, smaller than Sheba," I recite.

Papo slaps me across the face, and I taste warm and salty blood. My ears ring.

"Do it again," he commands the mage.

The mage stares at me with pitch-black eyes again as I think of the wall and how it reaches the skies. After three frustrating attempts, Papo orders Nasou to drag me back to my room. I wipe the blood on my lip with my hand.

"I'm sorry, Princess Nila," Nasou says as he opens the door to my room.

My left ear is ringing loudly, and I flop down on the floor and hug my knees. I knew this would come—I'd prepared myself for it. I'm going to be strong, and I won't break.

Papo would plunder Aksa and lay it to waste. Then he'd plunge the highlands into darkness with the magic called technology, and I don't want to imagine what he'd do if he ever heard of the forbidden weapons.

The next day, he asks the same questions, and I give the same answers. This time, Papo commands Nasou to take me to the dungeon cells instead of my room. The stink of the place clogs my nose, and I throw up in the corner. When I'd refused to tell him the truth, Papo had thrown his chalice at me, and now my forehead is bleeding, blood trickling down to my nose and lips.

In the dungeon cell, I spend the whole day and night on the cold hard floor, hearing the hopeless cries of the other prisoners.

"Nila?" a voice calls.

I stand up and walk to the bars to meet Kaku. I'm not feeling well, and I'm shivering. It feels good to see a familiar face.

"Oh, Nila, I'm so sorry this happened. How are you faring?" she asks, touching my face.

"I'm well," I say as I smile. I do not want to worry her.

"So what did you see in Aksa?" she asks, and I notice that her usually brown eyes are pitch black. I step back and head to the corner of the room. The person before me is no longer Kaku, but the mage.

"One way or another, I'm going to break you," he says before he disappears.

Chapter Twenty-One

I get chills thinking about what has just happened. I have to be careful. I cannot trust anyone. He could pretend to be anyone. A week passes by, and I get used to the smell of the vomit and the faeces in the dungeon cells.

Nasou sneaks me fresh bread and water every evening before the sun sets. The next day, he tells me I've been summoned, and I follow him. My whole body reeks. I've not bathed in a week.

Papo scrunches his nose when I come close.

"Nila, have you decided you will show me Aksa?" he asks, narrowing his eyes at me.

"Aksa is a humble kingdom. The people are farmers, and they value one another."

I flinch when he comes close. I'm expecting a slap, but it does not arrive.

"Very well. You have made your choice, and I have made mine. Tonight in the Great Hall, there will be a ceremony to celebrate the union of Sheba and Kush. I'm marrying off your sister Makeda to Prince Eshi," he says, pointing at Prince Eshi who is beaming from ear to ear. "Go to your room and get ready for the ceremony."

There is no way he will do it, will he? I think as I head back to my room. Makeda is only seven. She is a child. He is baiting me. When Neret brings bath water, I wash up quickly and eat the bread and chicken soup she has brought me. I've not had a warm meal in days.

When evening comes, I rush into the Great Hall and see servants setting up the food and wine for the preparations. I run back to Sahara's room and find no one. Where are my sisters? I do not find them in Kaku's room, either, and I start to panic. Maybe Papo meant what he said.

My body trembles as I walk back out and see my sisters being escorted into the Great Hall. Makeda is crying, wailing as she fights the guard dragging her in.

I walk back into the hall and find Papo and Prince Eshi already sitting down. Makeda is on his lap as she fights to get away from his grasp.

The mage sits next to Kaba, watching intently with pitch-black eyes.

"Nila, I reserved a seat for you." Papo points at a chair across from Prince Eshi where I can see him holding Makeda.

"You cannot do this. She is only seven," I say, watching Prince Eshi. If he lays a hand on her, I will cut his head off.

"Seven is a great age," Prince Eshi says, and I spit in his face.

"You've made your choice, girl," Papo snarls.

"Thank you Grand Emperor." Prince Eshi stands up. "I think we'll stay in early today." He motions for Makeda to stand up.

"You pig," I shout as he helps her stand up. I pick up a plate and throw it at him. Two guards restrain me from behind. Makeda is crying until snot runs down her face.

"I'll do it. Tell your mage I'll do it."

Chapter Twenty-Two

"Let Makeda leave, and I'll show you everything you want to see," I say, freeing myself from the grasp of the guards.

"Let her go," Papo says to a disappointed Eshi.

The mage approaches, and I sigh, my mind at the walls of Aksa. Slowly, the gate opens, and I try to show him as little as I can: the flower garden, the horse stables, and the green fields behind the flower gardens. But once he is in, he is too strong, and tears fall down my eyes as he breaks the thin barrier in my mind. He sees the palace, the technology, Seni's courtyard, and every moment I've shared with him.

"I'm sorry, Seni," I whisper to myself.

My lips tremble as I realize what I've just done. I'm the first outsider to enter Aksa, and I've let the worst people possible know what it looks like on the inside. After he's gone through every memory, the mage walks out, followed by Papo and Prince Eshi. I place my elbows on the long table then cover my face with my hands and cry.

I spend the night in the same position, long after everyone has left the hall.

"Wake up," a voice says, and I raise my head.

It's morning, and a guard is waking me up. I'm still in the Great Hall where I slept with my head on the hard table. My neck feels sore, and so does my throat. The pain and guilt in my heart are however more than the physical pain.

I slowly walk out of the Great Hall, looking at the surroundings of the palace. Life is going on as normal. I lean against a pillar, drop to the floor, and sit there. It is early morning, but the sun today is too hot as I feel it on my face and my back.

"Nila," Kaku calls as she helps me up. She helps me back to her room, and I lie down to rest my sore neck. "The grand emperor is leaving to attack Aksa. I heard him talk about it last night. He is going with the whole of our army, together with the mage, and the Kilishi," she says as she closes her door.

"It's all my fault. I wasn't strong enough," I say as I wipe away tears.

Papo has already told me I'd be part of the entourage leaving the next day for Aksa. From here, we can hear the marching of soldiers' feet as they assemble, ready to leave the next day.

"As soon as we leave, take my sisters to Tesfaye's sanctuary. I'll join you later," I urge her.

"I'll make sure they are fine," Kaku assures me. "I'm worried about you."

"I can take care of myself," I say as we hug.

We hear a scream and run out. Servants are crowding down at my mother's window. I rush forward to see her neck in an unnatural angle. There is blood running from her ear. Beru kneels beside her, crying. Kaku rushes to where she lies and touches her neck. I close my eyes as she tries to find a heartbeat.

Chapter Twenty-Three

Deep down, I know she is gone. I hold her cold hand as a guard carries her back inside to her room, where she loved spending her time. I'm in shock as Kaku wipes the blood on her face.

Before I left for Aksa, she'd come to see me and hugged Sahara and me. She may not have been present in our lives, but she was our mother. I feel sorry for her that this is her end.

"May the ascendants open the gates of Nahu for her," I say as I console Beru.

"There is blood under her fingernails," Kaku remarks, turning the nails over. I look around the room. She has a cut on the forehead, similar to mine when Papo's chalice hit me.

"What happened?" I ask Beru, who has gone to stand by the window and is crying softly. "Tell us the truth." I shake her by the shoulders.

"He...he came to see her. He said that he didn't need her anymore now he had a mage, and he was going to conquer Aksa," she says and stops as sobs rock her body. "She told him she was with child, and he said he didn't want another girl. Then she tried to grab his leg and plead with him, but he flung his wine cup at her. He told her to stand up and she did, and then he pushed her," Beru says, her eyes filled with fear. "Please don't tell anyone I told you. He'll have me killed." She kneels to beg me.

"Murderer!" I stand up, ready to face him in the throne room.

Kaku grabs my hand firmly. "Nila, don't. He might kill you, too."

I ball my fists. She is right. Now that Papo has his mage and has his army ready to fight in Aksa, he feels like he doesn't need anyone. I sigh. I'll find a way to avenge her death and that of my unborn sister or brother.

When Kaku finishes cleaning her, she binds her up, and a guard helps carry her down to the tombs where we lay her to rest. As we leave, I can hear her voice in my mind.

"*Everyone had to fulfil their role for Sheba.*"

The next morning at dawn, Nasou takes me to the fields where I see soldiers on horseback carrying Sheba's blue flags. There are archers with bows and arrows strapped on their backs. I think of the archer necklace deep inside my robes, my gift from Seni. That's the only personal thing I'm carrying, together with my little elephant carving, for good luck.

I estimate the whole of the army to be around seven thousand. I try to remember the number of

Seni's soldiers, but I cannot. I pray they're more than we are.

I catch my breath as I see soldiers emerge from the dungeons. They are grouped by two, and they carry hundreds of Kilishi in cages.

Chapter Twenty-Four

The journey is faster than I hoped it would be. The last time I travelled to Aksa, it took five days. Now, we are in Bazina by the fourth day and riding towards the wall. Papo rides in the front line, together with Prince Eshi and the mage.

I follow behind with King Mesati and the rest of the kings of Sheba.

After hours of riding, we arrive at the wall. I squeeze the elephant carving in my hand and pray to the stars that the mage fails. But then, I feel the ground rumbling, and I see the stones of the wall fall from the skies to the ground. The walls of Aksa are down.

When the dust and the rubble settle, we can see Aksa, and I hear Papo gasp as he stares at the palace.

"Flaming stars!" he says, his voice filled with awe.

I can feel the same excitement in the soldiers.

"You have no right of entry to Aksa," a voice says.

It's Seni, except I've never heard him sound so deathly before. He is standing in the front line with black gear and green, glowing shields. He looks straight at me, and his jaw ticks.

"I'm sorry," I whisper as I stare at his angry face. He'd invited me to his home, and here I was, back with an army to destroy everything he cared for. The hovering crafts stand all over the sky.

There is a roar of soldiers from both sides as they charge forward. I ride to the side, looking for somewhere to hide. I hear the snarl of the Kilishi as they are released from their cages and run into Aksa; I can hear screaming and roaring. I see Papo and the mage walk through the groups of fighting men heading towards the palace as smoke rises in the air.

I try to push myself forward, but there are fighting men everywhere. I search for Seni in the chaos, but I can't see him. I have to find him and fight with him. A solder knocks into me, and I fall, feeling a sharp pain in my left hip.

I stand up and try to forge forward when I see a flying spear headed towards me and I duck. Something hits me from behind the head, and I fall unconscious.

I don't know how long I'm down, but when I come to, there is smoke rising all over Aksa and piles of soldiers lying dead all over.

I drag my feet as I walk into Aksa. The flower gardens are burnt up, and there are dead bodies everywhere, as well as smoke from the hovering objects that have all fallen from the sky. I see the mage standing at the top of the stairs, his pitch-black eyes on me. He's laid this place to waste, and I helped him. I feel sick to my stomach.

I walk up the stairs. There are dead bodies sprawled all across the first three floors. There is no one I see on the fourth floor. It's empty. Seni's home is empty.

I make my way to the fifth floor. My heart beats fast as I see the man with the ochre-coloured locss dead on the floor of the courtyard. Seni's mother is lying in a pool of blood, and his father's body is next to hers, his hand stretched out as if he were crawling towards her.

I watch two Aksan men carry their bodies away.

Where is Seni?" I ask as they pass me and they freeze as if they had not realised I was there.

"Seni is dead."

I fall to my knees as I sob with my head hanging. I cry until my body trembles. I don't know how long I kneel there, but when I get up, it's dark. I head down to Seni's home. I clap my hands, and bright lights lit the house. There is a black boot on the floor in the hallway, as if he'd left in a hurry. I can smell him everywhere, in the rooms and the furs on the bed. I clutch them to my face and cry.

Afterward, I go to the tub and wash off the grime off my skin. I'd hurt my wrists and scraped my knees. My hip still hurt, and I'd twisted an ankle. The bath makes me feel better. I sit in the water, hug my knees, and cry more.

Then I get out, put on one of Seni's long robes, and sleep on his bed.

The following morning, I sit by the pool and feel the sun on my skin. Seni will never feel this again—he is dead. He didn't believe in the stars, too. He believed in a creator. I would not meet him in Nahu City in the afterlife. I'd never see him again.

There is a sound in the sky, and then, one of the objects he'd called the wings of justice drone floats directly at my face. This one is not smooth like an egg—it is square with red lights for eyes, and it has long metallic arms. Seni had told me it carried those who had committed unpunishable crimes to a crater past Mount Kosai and dropped them there.

It does not come as a surprise to me when it picks me up by the arms and flies me off to the mountains. I've committed an unpunishable offense by bringing invaders to Aksa. I deserve to die.

Chapter Twenty-Five

The cold numbs my skin, and I wonder what it will feel like when I plunge to my death. We fly past Mount Kosai and farther away into a range of smaller mountains. They are not small, but compared to Mount Kosai, they look like it.

The wings of justice drone hovers over the dark, bottomless hole, and I look down at the darkness. In the face of death, something inside me tells me to fight for my life. I try to wiggle out of the metallic arms, but it's futile, and even if I do, I'll fall straight down into the dark hole.

The object turns around and takes me back to where it took me from. I find one of Seni's cousins waiting for me.

I met him the first time I was here. I recognized the similar upturned eyes, but that's where the similarity ends. His locss fall to his ankles, and his ears are pierced. Big holes that would fit a coin from Sheba. I remember his name—Kashita, but he preferred to be called Kashi. I breathe when the wings of justice drone places me down on solid ground and flies off back to the mountains.

"You survived," I say, walking towards him and hugging him.

I expect him to push me away, but he does not. I know how it must seem to him, me in his cousin's home, wearing his robes. I'm an invader who has taken up everything for herself.

"I'm a coward who begged for his life." His shoulders drop. "And now, your father has put me in charge of teaching him about the magic of Aksa." His jaw ticks. "He has sent me here to summon you."

My shoulders are sore from where the metallic wings were holding me earlier.

"I have nothing to wear," I say, looking at the big robe on my body that is three times my size.

"Come." He sighs and leads me to the room I'd first used when I came to Aksa and opens a concealed door in the wall. Dresses of all colours and shapes hang inside.

"Seni made these so you'd find them ready for your next visit..." He closes his eyes as if remembering the exact moment. "See if there is something you like. If you don't, just press here. Choose something, and the 3D printer will do the rest."

He speaks rapidly as he presses on the wall. I look at the hanging clothes. Seni had been preparing for my next visit. I pick a bright orange. It's beautiful, but I don't feel like orange.

"I can't believe he is dead," I whisper as I run my fingers over the different fabrics. A tear falls on the dry clothes, and I wipe it off.

"Get ready. I'll be waiting outside," Kashi says.

I settle for black pants and a short cloak I'd heard Seni call a hoodie. The material of the pants snugs my skin, but it's still comfortable. I settle for black boots.

When I walk outside, Kashi is waiting for me, and we head below to the third floor.

"Teach my father as little as you can, if none at all," I say as we arrive at the throne room.

Papo is standing beside the large diamond throne which is carved from the same diamond of the palace. It is attached to it. He walks around it and looks up and down as he rubs his chin.

"Nila, did you learn how they carved these?"

"No," I say, looking at the mage whose magic I can feel crawling through my mind like a sharp finger bone.

"She tells the truth," the mage says.

His voice sounds like thunder, and the hair on my skin rises listening to him.

"It is only a matter of time before the rest of the highlands want Aksa for themselves," I say.

Papo stops walking around the throne and stares at me. I want him not to enjoy his victory and to never find comfort in Aksa for one single minute.

"They will come to fight you with full force, which is why you should rebuild the wall," I urge him. Kashi looks at me as if he can't decide what to think of me.

"Forget the wall. I'll fight them before they come for me," Papo says, looking under the hovering object that carries his wine chalice and follows him around.

This means he is leaving Aksa, and that might be an opportunity in itself. I stop thinking of how I'd use such an opportunity when I notice the mage staring at me. I have to find a way to block my mind from his reach.

For the next few weeks, the wings of justice drone comes for me every day and hovers me over the crater. As time goes, I don't feel as frightened. All I feel is anguish as I think of Seni and how I'm the cause of his death. I don't sleep well at night, and all I want to do is lie inside in the dark all day, but Papo's summons don't allow me to mourn in peace, as he calls for me at the most random times for the most mundane reasons.

"Nila," he says as I enter the throne room for the third time in the day. "Do you know this magic can tell me what time it is? I don't have to rely on the sun." He points at the tiny black band Kashi is putting around his wrist.

Everything about Aksa fascinates him, and after a lifelong search, he finds it is all worth it.

As I walk up the stairs, after leaving Papo to his marvels, I run into King Mesati who looks as weary as I am. He is wearing his war helmet and a breastplate.

"I thought the war was over," I say as I put my hands inside the jacket I'm wearing. I'm tired, and

I hope this was the last summon of the day so I can commiserate in peace and smell Seni's clothes.

"The grand emperor is sending me and the other kings, as well as some of his commanders, to Bazina. We are to start in the south in the Bairi region," he says as he readjusts his helmet.

The ache in my head fades away. Does this have anything to do with what I'd told him, that the rest of the highlands would attack? I only wanted him to feel miserable, and to prepare to defend Aksa.

"But the people in the Bairi region are just farmers. They are innocent. You cannot attack them on a whim." I follow him back down.

"Nila, when was the last time you saw me? I've been away for these missions for the past six weeks. We have been doing it for that long, and when we are done, we head to Pemba, and we stop when the rest of the highlands are subdued."

"These are innocent people. Innocent men, women, and children," I argue.

"I'm only a king. I follow the orders of my emperor wherever they may lead me."

I follow him back to the throne room. These innocent people do not deserve to lose their lives. I will say something to Papo about it even if it means he might have me lashed.

A guard runs past King Mesati and me and kneels at Papo's feet.

"Grand Emperor, we have received reports that there has been an uprising in Sheba. Hemi, the wine bearer, has declared himself the emperor of Sheba."

Mukami Ngari

Chapter Twenty-Six

Papo's eyes twitch as he stands up.

"That bastard. I should have killed him before he was born," he roars as he stands up and places his hands on his temples. "I will have his head rolling before the sun sets." He punches the arm of the diamond throne and massages his knuckles. "Mesati, you come with me. Let the rest proceed to Bazina." The hovering object follows behind with his wine. "We ride with two thousand men. Four thousand ride to Bairi with fifty Kilishi, and four thousand remain here in Aksa with the rest of the twenty Kilishi."

He'd lost thirty Kilishi during the war with Aksa.

"Papo, you cannot order attacks on these innocent people," I say, following him outside.

"Nila, if you say another word…" He leaves a threat hanging in the air. I watch as his soldiers assemble. He gets on his horse. "The mage will be in charge when I'm away. I'll be back in no time."

I watch as Papo rides past the crumbled-down wall and away. I walk back to Seni's house and find Kashi lying on the couch.

"I'm hiding from the voodoo guy."

"The mage?" I ask, standing by the table.

"Yeah. He keeps asking me to show him the magic that brought the people of Aksa here from the dying world. He means the time jump ship," he says, looking at the ceiling which shows a moving image of him and a beautiful, tall woman with short locss.

"You have to guard your mind. He can read minds. That's how he found out about Aksa. He broke into my head," I say, taking off my boots and holding them in my hand. I don't bother with the specifics of Makeda's wedding as it would make me cry.

When she comes to mind, I remember how much I miss my sisters. I've been too busy surviving, I've forgotten about them.

I wonder if they are still in Sheba or if they managed to go to Tesfaye's sanctuary. I know Kaku has done everything to protect them, and they must have left Sheba and are in the sanctuary now.

"So that's what happened," Kashi says. He waves his hand, and the paintings on the ceiling disappear. He sits up on the couch and looks at me again. "He's been trying to get into my head for weeks, but he's failed. I meditate every day. I will teach you how to block him out."

"I know how to block him out. I've done it before." I put my boots down and walk to the window. "When I returned home, Papo wanted to know what I'd seen in Aksa, but I wouldn't tell him the truth. He commanded the mage to read my mind, but I'd think of the high walls that protected Aksa," I say, enjoying the feeling of the cold floor on the soles of my feet. "He always failed. So Papo punished me and imprisoned me in the dungeons. But I didn't let the walls down. Then, he threatened to marry my sister Makeda, who is seven years old, to Eshi, the slave master. So I was let out of the dungeon to celebrate her marriage ceremony. That's when I let the walls down." I look over at Mount Kosai to see if the wings of justice drone can be seen.

"That is horrible. I'm so sorry." Kashi's eyes are filled with pity.

"I know how to block him out, but when I let the walls down, he went in, and I can feel him even now, crawling and scratching in my mind. I need to know how to kick him out again." I pause as the thought comes to mind. Then I take my boots and head to the door where I put them back on.

"Nila, where are you going?" Kashi asks, standing up.

"You come and see." I run out of the common room on the fourth floor, his feet tapping on the floor as he runs behind me.

When we reach outside to the stairs where the mage loves to stand, he stares at me with pitch-black eyes, and I narrow my eyes at him and concentrate. He flinches and waves his hands as if fighting something invisible.

"Are you doing that to him?" Kashi whispers.

"Yes." I chuckle.

The mage screams and runs back inside, and I can feel his hold on my mind weaken.

I'd thought of crows, tearing into his flesh, digging their blunt beaks into his skin as they ate him alive.

"You have to teach me how to do that. Did you see how he ran away?"

Kashi waves his hands in the air, imitating the mage, and we burst out laughing. I laugh until my ribs hurt. I look across the gates and see an envoy emerging from the mist. It's Prince Eshi who'd left after we arrived in Aksa.

He rides with two men in front, and behind them are close to thirty other men, all riding on horses. Judging from their light robes and turbans, they are from the desert, across the Qeyhlil Sea.

My laughter dies in my mouth. I have a feeling they do not come bearing good news.

Chapter Twenty-Seven

It doesn't take more than an hour before I'm summoned to the second floor. I kick and fight as a guard shoves me into a room. Prince Eshi and the two men from earlier are sitting inside.

The one in the middle has a big build, with thick brows, a large beard, and a scowl on his harsh face. His large, painted eyes cause chills to run down my back. Next to him is a lean, younger man with a softer face. I look at him, and he averts his gaze.

Five Aksan women are pushed into the room. The woman standing next to me is young, with braided hair and colourful beads that fall to her back. She reminds me of Sahara. Three other women join the line.

The big man stands up and examines us closely. He talks in a foreign language I do not understand. When he gets to me, he says something to Eshi who laughs.

"Nila, you go inside and wait for him," he says to me as he uses a stick to clean his teeth.

"You are crazy if you think I'll have to do anything you say." I narrow my eyes at them. "You are not in charge here. Papo is."

Eshi laughs as he stands up. The big man laughs, too, as the other one looks away.

"I'm not your father's dog. It's my mage who conquered Aksa. This is my empire, and I do what I want. You are all my slaves—you, your father, your grandmother, everyone in your lineage," he says as he touches my breast, and I slap his hand away.

He pauses, looks at me, then punches me hard in the gut until all air leaves my body. I backpaddle, and he kicks me on the chin. I fall, and he drags me by my leg to the bedroom as I fight him off.

Later that evening, I walk up to the fourth floor, stopping at each step to catch my breath and regain my strength.

"Princess." I hear Nasou's voice as I struggle to keep my eyes open. I need water, but the words don't come out of my mouth. Instead, I cough and see blood on my hand.

Nasou carries me the rest of the way into Seni's home. I rest on the bed as I hear him talking to Kashi. I want to cry, but there is no breath left in my lungs.

The next day, due to the serum Kashi gives me, I feel better, but I'm still sore. Most of the injuries have disappeared, but I remember everything.

I sit in the bath and cry for hours. I think about how it would feel if I stood at the edge of the pool and fell.

When I go back to the common room, Kashi silently hands me a glass of water. I take it as I sit down.

"He needs to be put to death." Kashi seethes. "I'm tired of these savage men getting away with everything. I'm going to kill him, Nila, you wait and see."

I haven't spoken a word since leaving that room. If I could, I'd say I agree.

I'll strangle Eshi with my bare hands.

"I'm so sorry, Nila, but I need your help for this to work. I'm sorry that I have to ask this of you. I know what you are going through."

"Name it," I say, my voice returning to me. It sounds hoarse, and I cough.

A few minutes later, I head outside. Across the palace stairs is a monument. It's tall and white, and the ground around it is red and circular. I stand there and clear my throat.

"Eshi," I call out to him. "Face me if you call yourself a man," I shout.

Inside, I'm shaking, hoping this works. He walks down the stairs, his friend beside him.

"I said, come and face me if you call yourself a man."

"Nila, if you wanted more of what you got last night, you should say so." He flexes his knuckles as he walks towards me.

He is so close to me, I can smell urine and sweat on him. He leers at me, and my voice fails.

My hands are trembling. He looks down and sees them—I hid them inside my pocket.

"You are stubborn. I'm going to enjoy breaking you," he says as he pinches me on my chin.

If Kashi was wrong, I'm done. I'd never survive another encounter with him again. He can smell my fear, and a wide grin spreads across his face. Then, the wings of justice drone hovers down and grabs him by his shoulders.

He screams as it carries him away, high up in the sky. I see it cross Mount Kosai and farther away. I breathe out. I see the mage watching me, and I wait for him to punish me for what I've done to his master. It is worth it, and if he kills me now, I'll have no regrets. The mage stares at me and walks away. Eshi's guest follows behind him.

"Are you alright?" Kashi asks as he comes to where I am.

The shaking in my body subsides.

"How did you do that?" I ask, walking away from the red square.

"It's an intelligent machine. I sent it an alert of an unforgivable crime that has happened. It analysed the details and concluded on Eshi."

I'm still shaking as we walk back into Seni's home. Hearing a sound coming from across the hallway, I open Seni's bedroom and go out onto the balcony.

The wings of justice drone is floating outside, alone. It dropped Eshi into the dark hole. It stares at me for a while and then flies away.

Chapter Twenty-Eight

The next day, I decide to stay inside. The books on Seni's shelves are written in a language I do not understand, but I flip through one of them, trailing the foreign symbols with my fingers.

I imagine if he were here, we'd be sitting on this chair. I'd be on his lap, and his hand would be caressing the small of my back as he teaches me the symbols.

Kashi stumbles in through the door and paces around the room. I put the book down.

"I heard those guys out there say that you were leaving with them tomorrow. Those friends of that man, the slave master."

I stand up. Eshi's friends from across the Qeyhlil Sea. I know they are not taking me along for companionship. I'll be traveling as a slave.

"You have to leave. We have to get you out of here," he says. "I heard wagons are leaving for Bazina, with food and supplies for the soldiers who are fighting in the Bairi region. We have to get you on one."

I stand there looking at him. He spins me into action and leads me inside, hands me a linen dress and cloak, and brown boots.

"These will help you blend in with the rest of the outsiders."

I change as he walks into the other room, and notice the soles of both my feet have turned black as I put on the boots.

Kashi comes back with a pouch and gives it to me.

"These are a hundred and one diamonds. If you trade one, you can find your way out of the highlands." He places it in my hands.

"I cannot take them," I say, handing them back to him.

"Nila, take them, they are yours. Seni was going to give them to you, on the day he proposed marriage to you," Kashi says, folding my hand around my palm.

I nod and put it deep in the pocket of my robe. Seni was going to ask me to marry him. I think of it as we sneak out of the palace and down into the stables where the wagons line up. Kashi helps me into one of them and covers me with a sack.

"Stay quiet until you leave Aksa, then you jump and run."

"Thank you, Kashi," I say, grabbing his arm. "I'll never forget this."

I lie and wait. The hours pass by, and I wonder if we will be leaving at all. Then at dawn, we begin moving. I keep my head down as the rider greets the soldiers manning the crumbled entrance.

I hear the horse trot down the road, and we ride for hours. I take a peek outside, and from the position of the sun, I can see it's noon.

When we stop, I hear the man whistling. I peek as he disappears into a thicket of bushes, then I rise and get out of the wagon.

I take off running. In the opposite direction. I know we are in Bazina. I try to find any familiar hills, but I see none. I will keep on walking until I'm far away from the south.

I hold on to a tree to catch my breath, then keep walking. There is a river nearby, and I stop to drink water.

I hear the rustling of leaves and stand, coming face to face with Kaba, the wizard.

I haven't seen him a lot since the mage took his place. I wonder where he has been all this time. I cross the shallow river and keep running.

"Nila, wait!" He pursues.

I run faster and look back to see him behind me. If he catches me, he'll drag me straight back to Papo. I won't let that happen, not now when true freedom is within my grasp, and I'm this close to reuniting with my sisters.

He is gaining ground, and he pulls at my cloak. I take the diamond pouch inside my pocket and let the cloak slip off me into his grasp.

"Stop," he snaps.

I look back to see him, trailing too close to me. I stumble and fall, and he catches up with me.

I can't let him take me back. I have to stop him.

A whooshing sound comes from the sky, and a flaming stone falls between us, scorching the green grass and turning the soil black.

Kaba stares at the rock and then at me. I stand up and run, but he does not pursue me further.

I walk until sunset and stop to rest my burning feet. I look at the pouch in my hand—I cannot keep walking around carrying it. I look for a gum tree and use the sticky gum to stick the little stones at the front of my body.

I stick them around my chest and my breasts, all around my belly and on my thighs.

I'll keep them on me till I can purchase another cloak. I need a cloak as the cold is biting.

From the cover of the trees, I see a downtrodden path and decide to follow it. I hear the sound of hoofs, and before I can bolt back into the forest, I see five riders. I recognize them immediately—I'd seen them before on my first visit to Aksa.

I remember the beautiful woman with blue braids; her name was Zeli. She alights off her horse and walks to me.

"If it isn't the princess of Sheba." She smiles. She has a short, blunt weapon in her hand, and she places it against my neck.

A painful tremor runs through my body. My heart pounds fast, and I feel like it might explode.

I flop down like a sack of grain and float in and out of consciousness.

"You didn't have to taser her," a man says as he picks me up.

"Relax, she'll be fine. Let's take her back to camp."

Chapter Twenty-Nine

When I open my eyes, I groan from the pain in my neck. We arrive at their camp. It's expansive, littered with various sizes of tents, all black. There must be over seven thousand people here.

I see men women and children in some of the tents, and I also see soldiers make way for us as we walk through. There are no smiling faces. If they pounce on me, not even a drop of my blood would reach the ground.

My throat grows dry as Zeli pushes me forward to the big black tent in the centre.

"Arms and legs apart," she orders as she pats me down from head to toe. She pauses around my chest and my belly. "Anything you'd like to let me know?" she asks, narrowing her eyes at me.

"Diamonds," I say, holding my chin up.

She takes a peek inside my dress and looks away, then disappears inside the tent and re-emerges after a while. She shoves me inside where it's dimly lit with a lamp by the entrance and one in the middle.

There is a man inside, standing in the dark corner. He is wearing black pants and a turban around his head. His upper body is bare. He is standing with his back to me. He is huge, and I can see every muscle honed by training. A scar runs from his waist going all along to his front. I wish he'd turn around and I'd see where it ends.

"Look, if it's about the diamonds, you can have them all. Nobody needs to get hurt," I say, rubbing my sweaty palms on my dress.

He turns around and starts walking towards me, and I peddle backwards.

"You mean my diamonds."

That voice! I gasp as he takes of his turban and a stray locs falls across his perfect face. I want to lock it behind his ear, but I'm stuck in place, paralysed in fear.

"It's been too long, Princess," Seni says as he holds up my chin.

"You are alive," I say, tears falling down my eyes. I crash into him, my face buried into his chest.

When I pull back, he is standing there unmoved, an unreadable expression on his face.

"I hear you have something that belongs to me," he says, his eyes on my dress, which hides the diamonds, all a hundred and one of them.

"They were given to me," I say as I swallow.

"They are mine, and I don't remember giving them to you. Let's see them."

I slowly drop the dress. It falls over my shoulders and then down, exposing my breasts and belly. It only covers my bottom half now.

"Don't be shy. It's nothing I haven't seen before," Seni says as he raises his brow.

I drop the dress and stand naked before him. He taps his finger on his chin as he examines each of the stones that glitter in the night light.

"You have a talent for smuggling, Princess. This is creative."

He picks the first diamond off my chest. His finger brushes against my skin, and I swallow. He takes off another diamond from the space between my breasts, then moves to the ones I'd patched around my left breast.

"These come from some of the deepest mines in Aksa."

His thumb brushes against my nipple as he takes off another one, and I gasp.

He takes a pouch from his pockets and puts them inside. Then he moves over to my right breast, and I swallow. There are too many diamonds left, and if his fingers brush against me like that again, I might throw myself at him.

"Stop squirming," he says as he picks the last diamond from my nipple. He squats down so his face is on my belly. "Let's see what you have here."

I can feel his breath on my skin.

"My little beauties," he says as he holds another one in the light before placing it in the pouch.

He has an edge to him, a fierceness that wasn't there before he left, and I realise the scar from his waist ends at his chest.

He looks as good as I remember, and I catch my breath when he lifts up my chin so I can look into his honey-coloured eyes which are filled with contempt, for me.

"I want you to watch me take back everything you stole from me," he says as his eyes pin me down. "I'm going to enjoy making you pay, Princess."

He leaves the tent, and I pick my dress back from the ground, put it on. I sit down on the bed and thank the stars. Seni is alive. I hear a loud bang outside, and I stand up to peer outside the tent.

I see men, women, and children gather around Seni who is on top of his stallion. His soldiers are already surrounding him, and I estimate eight hundred warriors. They are wearing full body armour, and each one of them is carrying the forbidden weapon of the dying world called guns.

"Aksans," Seni begins his address. "We have come a long way, and tonight, we take back what is rightfully ours."

His warriors roar, and I feel the hairs on my arms rising.

"The Grand Emperor of Sheba took our home, slaughtered our women, and butchered our children," he says as he looks at me. "Tonight, we fight in the name of every man, woman, and child who lost their life. Tonight, we pay that debt of blood with blood. Tonight, we fight in the name of my father, Emperor Teti, and my mother, Empress

Nakaaba. Tonight, we take back the empire of Aksa."

The people clap and shout as the warriors start marching.

His eyes lock with mine, and he rides towards me. He gets off his horse and stalks into the tent, picking his gun from the corner where he stands.

"Seni, you said it is an unforgivable offense to use the weapons," I say as I walk into the centre of the tent. He'd told me of the trouble they'd caused in the dying world.

"That was before my mother died in cold blood," he says as he faces me.

"It will cause great harm. Innocent people will lose their lives. If you do this, you will be no better than him." I stand my ground.

"I'll do whatever it takes to win this war," he replies before stalking out of the room.

I stay in the tent, my thoughts consuming me. With Papo's mage and Seni's forbidden weapon, the highlands would soon be plunged into a period of darkness. I lie down, then I stand up and pace around, as there is not much to do, and there is a guard stationed outside the tent at all times.

"You, out," Zeli commands as she stands by the door.

I follow her out to find a group of fifteen soldiers waiting for me.

"Death to Sheba." A man with red-coloured locss spits at me. He pushes me to the ground, and I fall into the mud.

"Our families were killed, and Aksa was conquered because of you, Sheba." Zeli sneers.

They tie me to a post and start shooting arrows at me, and they laugh each time I flinch. I'm saved when it starts to rain hard and they head back to their tents and leave me outside in the rain. It falls hard on me until I'm soaking and shaking. A woman with silver locss unties me, and I head back to the tent.

I dry myself up and cover myself with the furs. I wonder if Seni and his soldiers are fighting in this weather.

The weather remains dull for the next four days, and it saves me from being used as a practice target. The guard makes sure to hand me bread and stew the woman with the silver locss shares with me. I take the time to rest. In Aksa, I'd not been able to sleep well. I was grieving Seni, and I was always being summoned by Papo. Now, under the lure of the rain, I sleep in and relax. I wake up, eat and drink, then sleep.

"They are back!" Zeli shouts as she runs across the camp. "Seni is back!"

I get out of the tent and watch as Seni's men return to camp. There are shouts of joy as they ride in. The heads of the Sheba commanders are stuck on tree pikes, and the Aksa flags fly high.

Seni rides in the centre, and the people of Aksa leave their tents and welcome him.

"Long live Emperor Seni!" they chant and shout.

Emperor—he got Aksa back. I smile.

Outside, the singing and dancing gets louder. I can hear the rhythmic lilt of the qanun and the hum of the goblet drums, the stomping of feet, the accompanying whistling and clapping.

The festivals continue late into the night, and I can even hear children outside playing.

From what the guards outside are saying, Seni defeated Papo and his army and pushed them out of Aksa. The Grand Emperor, after reconquering Sheba, had returned to Aksa. At first, Papo had been confident he'd win the war until he saw Seni shoot his mage on the leg with a gun. The mage had limped away out of Aksa, screaming. Seeing that Seni's weapon could injure even a mage, Papo had lost confidence and fled back to Sheba, together with his army. I laugh so hard until tears fall down my eyes as I imagine the mage screaming and limping away.

At some time after midnight, Seni walks in. He is still wearing his war armour, and he still has blood, mud, and grime on his face. I can see little fresh cuts on his face. I sit up and look at him.

He sits on the chair next to my bed. I see blood stains on one of the diamonds on the crown on his head. If I could paint, I would paint him like this. He reflects everything light and dark inside of him—beauty, power, fury, and strength.

"Have you ever danced for a young emperor before?" he asks, and I feel every inch of my skin heat up.

I remember Dalia's lessons as I straddle him on his chair and take off his armour, brushing my fingers against his skin.

I move to the rhythm of the drums outside. I move my belly and my arms like a serpent and put him into a trance. He is mine, and in this beautiful nightmare, he is alive, and we are here together.

I know he hates me, but if my heart could speak, it would sigh his name over and over again. I love him, insane as it might be.

Outside, the people sing praises for their young, victorious emperor as he grabs me and my legs circle around his waist as his hot mouth finds mine. Our tongues intertwine as we kiss, fast and urgent, and I hold on tight to him as I yield my mouth to him. He grazes my bottom lip, and I whimper. I can feel his hard sex prick against my belly, and I wiggle to angle myself. He curses under his breath and tosses me aside before leaving the tent.

I lie down, frustrated. I don't see him again until the next morning as the camp disbands and we ride to Aksa.

The people of Aksa follow behind, raising purple flags high up in the air. Sheba's blue flags are defaced, most trampled upon, and the people lay them on the ground for Seni's horses to step on.

I keep my gaze on the road ahead as the whispers about who I am grow louder.

"Death to Sheba!" They point at me as I pass by, and sneer. Someone throws a stone at me, and it lands on my jaw, and I almost fall from my horse. The guards on both of my sides shield me the rest of the way.

Chapter Thirty

When we get to the crumbled walls of Aksa, Seni gets off his horse and looks around at the rubble. The flower gardens are destroyed, scorched to the ground, but some have started to bloom again. Some diamond statues have been plundered, others defaced. The gold-paved streets have been robbed and dismantled.

Kashi is waiting for Seni at the bottom of the stairs and welcomes him with a hug.

"I wish to be left alone," Seni says as he walks to the underground floors where his parents' tombs are. He takes off the crown from his head as he walks down the spiral of stairs.

"Let's go." Kashi whisks me away, and we go back to Seni's home.

I don't know if I'm still welcome. I use the room I was using while here. Outside the window, I watch Seni in the flower gardens kneeling before a statue of his parents. It has been defaced and misses their hands which were clasped together. He stays there on his knees until evening. I wish I could go to him, hold his hand, and wipe his tears, but I'm part of the reason they are not here. I brought war to his gates.

As the days go by, Seni is busy as he oversees the rebuilding of the walls. We haven't been alone ever since the night in the tent when he tossed me on the bed and walked away. His coronation is in three days, and there is a lot of activities going on.

With Seni occupied, Zeli targets and taunts me every moment she gets. No matter how much I stay away from her, each time I l bump into her, she always has something to say.

"Soon, we are marching to war, and we will lay Sheba to waste," she says as she laughs.

"So you've told me." I sigh.

"Emperor Seni wants you to see it all with your eyes, and then after that, your head shall be his."

"Every part of my body is his." I wink at her, leaving her and her companion dumbfounded as I walk back into Seni's home.

Kashi had showed me how to conjure up instruments with technology. When I get to my room, I conjure a beautiful harp and start playing. Back in Sheba, I used to love playing the harp, when I was young.

I think of the moment Zeli talks about. I'm tired of being reminded that I shall die by Seni's hand. Will the last thing I see in this world be honey-coloured eyes? I wonder if he'll make it quick, and what weapon he'll use. Will he smile?

I'll definitely cry, not from the wound inflicted, but from the breaking of my stupid heart.

There is a knock on the door, and I stop playing. I open it, and a liquorice scent wafts in as Seni enters.

The night light makes his eyes sparkle. He stands majestic, and a well-sculpted body is visible under his pants and shirt. I can't blame myself for falling for him.

"You play the harp well." He paces around the room, looking around at everything but me.

"Thank you."

'My coronation is in three days. There will be a lot of people present...would you prefer to stay here for your own safety, or do you want to come? I'll ensure enough safety for you."

His hands are behind his back as he looks outside the window.

"I want to come," I say as I massage my index finger which is sore from playing the harp.

"Alright." He turns and heads out the door.

On the day of Seni's coronation, I stand among the people of Aksa at the bottom of the stairs to the palace. There are people everywhere I turn. All of Aksa showed up for this event, some stand outside the gates. Because of the way I was treated along the roads as we came to Aksa, Seni has stationed six soldiers to guard me.

According to their culture, an Aksan emperor is crowned on Mount Kosai, by six elders and twelve kings, then they fly down to the palace where they meet their people and receive their good wishes in the throne room.

"Here they come," one of the guard says. The people begin to cheer and clap.

Seni descends and waves to the people. He looks dashing in the purple royal robes, and he holds a diamond-encrusted sceptre similar to his father's, which was looted by Papo.

The procession is heavily guarded. His soldiers walk beside him on foot while others ride on horses, and others fly.

"I can't believe it's finally happening," someone next to me says amidst the crowd's claps and cheers.

Seni passes by, waving at the people, and goes inside the throne room with the kings of Aksa. The royal households file in first to pledge their allegiance to Seni who sits on a diamond-encrusted throne.

Cheers turn into murmurs as people point at the halfway built gates. I turn around to see King Mesati and the rest of the kings on horseback. They alight and are immediately surrounded by archers.

Chapter Thirty-One

Seni leaves the throne room and goes to meet them. I move closer so I can hear every word said.

King Mesati takes a step forward and bows. "Emperor Seni, long may you reign. My name is King Mesati."

"What do you want?" Seni asks in a clipped tone.

"Emperor Seni, I speak on behalf of the kings of Sheba to let you know that we pledge our allegiance to you. We wish to formally announce that in the coming war, we will fight on your side against Grand Emperor Nefe."

My heart pounds fast as I watch the exchange. There is going to be another war. Regaining Aksa was not the final war—Seni wants to make sure he crushes Papo, and Papo wants a second chance to regain Aksa.

"I don't need your support. I have all the support I need, and how can I trust kings who desert their emperor?"

"Emperor Seni, you ask a very valid question. We are not deserting the grand emperor. We are doing this because we love Sheba. The grand emperor must be stopped. If not, he will be the downfall of the Sheba Empire. We believe you will win the war, and with your help, we can regain Sheba, and you can continue leading Aksa in peace, without interference as the emperors before you."

"You must think I'm foolish. I know all about Sheba's cheap tricks. Take them away."

Within seconds, they are surrounded and taken away to be locked up.

The commotion dies, and the line files forward. When it's my turn, I get on my knees like everyone else before me and pledge my allegiance.

"Long may you reign, Emperor Seni."

I'm aware the throne room has grown quiet and all eyes are on me. Seni is supposed to tell me to rise so I can leave, but he doesn't say a word. I'm not supposed to look up at him, but I do.

"Rise," he finally says.

I leave, the tail of my purple dress sweeping the floor behind me. Later, when the royal families go to celebrate in the Great Hall, I'm escorted by three guards back to my room. I'm exhausted—I bet a thousand people killed me in their heads today.

I soak in the tub as I think about what Sheba's kings did. They finally deserted Papo. It must have taken a lot of courage for King Mesati to convince the rest, as I'm sure he's the one who did. I hope Seni doesn't kill them; I'd hate to see King Mesati's head on a pike.

When night comes, I sit at the window and watch the bright, shining stars in the sky. There is a knock on my door, and it startles me back to reality.

I open the door, and Kashi is standing outside. "King Mesati asked me to deliver a message to you."

"Is he alright...what is Seni going to do to them?" I implore.

"They are being held until we ascertain where their loyalty lies." He looks at the harp in the corner of the room.

"What was his message?" I ask.

"He says that I should tell you that after your sisters left for the sanctuary, your sister Sahara came back to Sheba with Kaku to try and find a way to come to you, but she was detained by your father and is to married to Fesi in three days."

My knees feel weak, and I lean against the door.

"Who is Fesi?" Kashi asks as he holds me up.

"A warlord. I need to get back to Sheba." I walk across from my room, stumble down the hallway, and knock on Seni's room.

I open the door and walk in. He is sitting by his bedside table in nothing but pants as he reads from a book and writes down.

Kashi catches up with me, but I'm already inside. He retreats and leaves me alone with Seni.

"I have to go back to Sheba," I say, my voice trembling.

"Does this have to do with King Mesati's message?" Seni asks as he puts his book down.

I attempt to speak, but a sob wracks through my body. I wipe fresh tears from my eyes and nod instead.

"Yes, I need to go home right away."

I sob into my palms. I cannot even bring myself to think what Sahara would go through. Prince Eshi is nothing compared to Fesi, the bringer of death. He plunders villages, rapes women, and kills children for pleasure. I don't know where Papo finds these suitors. I have to stop the wedding before it happens.

"I want to help you, Nila." He removes my hands from my face. "Kashi told me everything about what you've endured under your father, how you were forced to reveal Aksa to save your sister, and what that Prince Eshi did." He balls his feasts. "I'm sorry, Nila. I've been wondering why he has not sent anyone to negotiate for your release. I've waited, but so far, no one has come. You could be dead by now, but he hasn't bothered to look for you. He does not care for you." Seni's nostrils flare. "What is your plan after you go back to Sheba?"

"I want to take her away, back to where my other sisters are. I met a man, an astrologer who has created a sanctuary Papo can never find."

"Is it Tesfaye?"

"Yes. Do you know him?"

"Yes. He is a good man. You can trust him, and I've seen the sanctuary. I'll help you get them there. Sleep. We will talk about it tomorrow."

"Thank you." I can breathe easy now.

When I go back to my room, I cannot sleep, and I play the harp until dawn.

The next morning, I wait for Seni as he returns from sparring in the courtyard with Kashi.

"The best entry point to the palace of Sheba is the western gate," I narrate as we walk towards the horse stables. "Here, below the cover of trees, is a tunnel that leads to the healers' quarters. From there, Kaku will be able to help. She is like our second mother."

I'm so eager to get my sister out, I haven't eaten since waking up. "In my room, there is a chest of gold coins concealed under the floor. I saved it when I was in charge of trading spices. She can carry it. It will be enough to sustain them for a while before I join them."

"You don't have to worry about that. I'll make sure she is well taken care of. Five trackers will be enough to get them out of the palace. I'll send them in two days," he assures me as we walk towards the new walls that were almost done.

"Thank you, Seni. My sisters are everything to me."

I don't care who is watching, I fling my arms around him and hug him. I'm so excited, I could kiss him. He puts his arm around me and pulls me close.

He keeps his word, and two days later, I watch as the trackers leave under his command. I pray to the stars everything will go according to plan.

"It will work out, don't worry about it," Seni says as he stands beside me. He escorts me back to my room. "I'll see you tomorrow," he adds as he stands and straightens his robes.

"Stay a little longer, please." I reach for his arm, pulling him down to the bed with me.

He obliges, and we sleep side by side, his hands around my waist. My back rests against his muscular chest. I yawn as I close my eyes and sleep.

Chapter Thirty-Two

Seni is already gone when I wake up. I feel lighter and happier than I'd ever been in years. After having my morning meal, I hum as I stroll towards the flower gardens. I see Seni coming from his parents' tomb and smile, hastening my step. When our eyes lock into each other, he walks in the opposite direction. I notice he is avoiding me, and to save myself the embarrassment, I stick to my room.

I don't know what has changed. I thought we'd made progress. Maybe he'd reconsidered being close to me. I wouldn't blame him. My stupid heart aches, and I play the harp for her to mend faster.

"I've been sent by Seni to tell you that your sister has arrived well in the sanctuary." Kashi delivers the message to me outside the door of my room.

It's been a week since the trackers left. Thank the stars, the plan worked, and they are all safe now.

"Tell him I said thank you." *Why has he been avoiding me like a plague?*

Kashi nods. "He also said I should tell you that we leave for Sheba in three days."

I feel chills on my skin. The time has come, and we are riding home to Sheba for the ultimate battle.

The day finally comes, and we begin to march. The ride back home to Sheba is a blur to me. It rains a lot along the way, and every part of me is drenched in rain. My cloak is soggy, and my fingers feel numb, but it did not outmatch what I feel deep down. My spirits are low, and my heart cannot get over Seni's rejection. Even as we camp, he makes sure we don't cross paths.

After five days of riding, we arrive, and I can see Papo's palace on top of the hill.

I've known this place as a comforting home when I was a little girl and as a heavily guarded prison when I became a woman.

Papo and his men are lined up in front of the palace gates, and he rides in front with his mage.

"Princess."

Seni calls me to the front, and I go to him. This is the first time we've stood close to each other since the night he slept in my room.

He gets off his horse and faces me, the flaming torches his men hold shining in his honey-coloured eyes.

"He dies today," he declares. "I never got the chance to say farewell to my father, but I won't deny you that chance. Go, see him one last time."

He kisses me on the forehead.

I look past him, at his men carrying guns and the kings of Sheba who now fight with him.

I walk uphill towards home, then turn and look back at Seni. There was a time I'd dreamt he would come riding through the gates for me. He stands here now, and he brings war and death with these forbidden weapons. He is back on his black stallion, wearing his black war attire, and the look in his eyes sends a chill down my bones.

I get closer to Papo. He's lost a lot of weight. His pot belly looks like a pouch, his balding hair thin and dry. His attire looks shabby, as if he's slept in it.

"Papo...Surrender, and end this war. So many lives have been lost already."

It feels like I've gone mad because I can hear the wailing of mothers and the cries of children who've lost their loved ones and their homes because of Papo's ambitions. There has been carnage across the highlands. I can hear the dead souls crying for vengeance. They scream for me to avenge them and ask me to end this. They want me to condemn him to darkness and desolation. They call this justice.

"You have chosen your side, whore of Sheba, and I have chosen mine," Papo says.

The look in his eyes breaks me. He is never going to change; he cannot be redeemed. He raises his bow and arrow at me, and the voices grow louder. I'm the one to do it.

"Stop!" The word comes out of my mouth, but the voice sounds nothing like me. It sounds like a storm, and it reverberates across the palace grounds.

I feel a dull pain in my eyes, and I scream. When open my eyes again, Papo's widen in horror. I know what he sees—my eyes glow white.

"I curse your soul. Let it be destroyed now by the light of the celestial city. You are never to be reborn as a mortal again. All you will know is darkness," I say as a shooting star falls at the speed of light.

When it gets near, it appears like a flaming rock the size of a man's head, and it's heading straight at Papo. He looks up at the sky and then back at me, his mouth wide open as the flaming rock hits him in the chest and he falls down, a hole burning through his body.

He is dead, gone. The mage looks at me with pitch-black eyes as another ball of fire sinks into his skull.

My hands hold on to the arrow stuck in my gut. Papo had fired the arrow as he fell. I see a big patch of fresh blood on my cloak as I fall down. I try hard to breathe, but the air feels thick, and I can't take it in.

I hear screaming as more rocks fall all around me. My eyes feel heavy, and I look at the sky and pray to the stars to give me a bit more time. The last thing I want to see is honey-coloured eyes.

"Nila." Seni kneels beside me, his hands applying pressure on my wound.

I smile, looking at his eyes as everything fades, and all that remains is darkness.

Chapter Thirty-Three

I'm standing at the banks of a river. I don't know how I got here. All I know is that I can't leave. I have to wait.

At last, a boat appears in the horizon, glowing stars all around it. The rider is seven feet tall, and his eyes glow a golden hue.

"Star Summoner, do not fear. I'm an ascendant, and I'm here to take you to Nahu, the celestial city," he says.

He is wearing a black cloak. The wind around us is fierce, but his cloak never flutters.

"Come," he says, extending his hand to me.

Don't let them do this to you again. Jump into the river. Jump now.

I look at the Ascendant and then at the river. Then I jump, and it feels like a thousand hands are pushing me back. It hurts, and I scream as I move fast, down to the bottom of the river. It hurts to be pushed back like that.

I open my eyes. My whole body is sore. I sit up and look around. I'm in Sheba, back in my room. I panic, but then I see Seni, sleeping on a chair next to my bed.

With great difficulty, I take off one of the linen sheets off my bed and drape it around him.

Shebiku walks in. I haven't seen him since the first time I visited Aksa.

"Sssh." I don't want to wake up Seni. He nods and walks to me, examines my eyes, ears, and tongue, then he unties the bindings around my belly.

"Where have you been?" I whisper as Shebiku gives me a cup of water which I gobble.

"Deep in the mountains in my research laboratory. I'd asked not to be disturbed for three months. Imagine my shock when I emerged from my cave five days ago to the news of everything that has happened," Shebiku says in a low tone as he hands me a glowing green liquid. I take it in my hands, enjoying the warmth down my throat but hating the bitter taste.

Seni opens his eyes, and he looks straight at me as I take a sip of the medicine. He is beautiful, and my heart skips. I'm mesmerised, like the first time we met.

"Good morning, Emperor." I smile, my voice a little hoarse.

He does not answer but stares at me intently. Stunned.

Then he hugs me. My ribs ache, and the hot green liquid sloshes on my thighs.

"Be careful, cousin," Shebiku urges as he re-enters my room.

Seni kisses my cheeks, and both his hands hold the sides of my face as he looks me in the eye.

"I thought I'd lost you." He touches his forehead to mine.

"How do you feel, Nila?" Shebiku asks.

"I feel great," I say, my forehead still linked with Seni's.

"You know I'm a science man. I don't believe in magic, but I hear you can control meteors. Would you mind if I studied your brain, purely for research purposes?" Shebiku asks as he takes away the empty cup which held glowing green liquid.

"Shebiku," Seni warns as he glares at his cousin.

Shebiku raises his hands up in defence. "Message received, Emperor."

He examines my body once again and gives me another bitter drink. Three sips in, and I fall back asleep.

When I wake up, it's dark. A lamp lights the room. Seni is sitting next to me.

"How are you feeling?" He helps me sit up.

"Famished. I could eat a whole cow."

"Shebiku says you can only eat soup. Wait here." He stands up, then comes back with a bowl of soup and starts feeding me.

"I can feed myself, you know. My arms are still working."

"Save your energy so you can heal faster." He gives me another spoonful of chicken soup.

"How long has it been since…since I was wounded?" I ask as I chew.

"It's been three days." Seni dabs the corners of my mouth with a white linen cloth.

In my dream, it had felt like a few hours.

"Papo's dead," I say as I bite my lip. I wonder if I imagined it.

"Yes." Seni watches me chew and swallow.

"I want to see him," I say as I try to get off the bed. My legs are stiff.

"Nila, you have to recover first," Seni says as he puts the bowl of soup down.

I get off the bed and sit back down. I'm too weak.

"I can walk," I argue as he carries me up the stairs, to Papo's room.

"Are you sure you want to see him? I think you should wait."

"I'm sure."

He sets me down, and I hold on to him as we walk inside. Papo's body is laid on the bed. The hole through his body has a ring of black all around it.

"I did this to him," I whisper as my lips tremble.

The ascendant had called me a star summoner. I'd summoned a star and burnt a hole through Papo's body.

"We will figure it out together." Seni squeezes my hand.

I take the wine chalice on Papo's bedside table and place it in his hands. He never parted from that chalice.

Seni holds to my side as we go down the stairs. I feel faint, and my knees almost buckle up. At the bottom of the stairs, in front of the throne room, stand the twelve kings of Sheba. King Mesati walks towards us carrying Papo's crown.

He kneels before me and extends Papo's gold crown to me. "Long live Nila, empress of Sheba."

"Long live, Empress," the other kings' echo, as they kneel before me one by one.

Chapter Thirty-Four

"Empress?" I ask Seni once the kings leave the throne room.

It has never occurred to me I'd ever become empress of Sheba. I'd thought Papo would live forever.

How am I supposed to run a whole empire?

"We will learn together. I'm also learning how to govern Aksa," Seni says as he rubs my back.

"There's the whole star summoning gift I have to figure out, too. I can't be an empress," I say as I fold my arms.

"Listen to me," Seni says as he takes my hand. "No one is better suited to rule Sheba than you are."

He kisses the top of my head as we head back to my room.

"What are we going to do about Aksa? So many people know about it now." I ignore a dull ache in my belly.

"Well, you will find out that many people are already forgetting what they saw or heard we are conducting a mass memory wipe," Seni says as he opens the door to my room.

"I don't want to forget," I say as I get on the bed. I can already feel the effect of Shebiku's serums.

"You won't forget a thing." Seni places the fur cover over my body.

I immediately drift off to sleep, the physician's potions still in effect.

In the weeks that follow, I continue to recover with the help of Shebiku. When I look in the mirror, I do not see glowing eyes. I see a face that has lost weight, and cracked lips.

If Dalia could see me now. I wonder where she is. I have not seen her and Nasou anywhere. I should have run into them by now.

I sit by the window and watch as servants clear up what had been ravaged by the flaming stars. There is debris, blood, and broken glass everywhere. I learnt thirty-four people lost their lives that day. They'd died by my hand. I've seen their faces, and the damage I've caused, and it's something that will torment me for as long as I live. It's only fair I live with this guilt.

On most days, I stay in my room, where Seni has set camp, as well. He is staying in Sheba for a few weeks and will then go back to Aksa after I'm crowned empress. At night when he thinks I'm asleep, he takes off his robes and works in his pants.

The weather in Sheba is particularly warm at this time of year. From where I lie on the warm bed, I see his muscular back as he studies the records of the previous Emperors of Aksa. I want to trace every muscle. I need him, because I'm afraid to fall asleep. When I close my eyes, I dream of the Ascendant and his glowing eyes judging me, telling me I cheated death, and that it will find me.

The next day, I'm surprised to wake up and see my sisters surrounding my bed. Seni had wanted it to be a surprise. They look healthy, happy, and beautiful. They are all here except Sahara who has decided to stay back at the sanctuary with the astrologers. I respect her choice, but I miss her. I wonder what made her stay away. Did anything happen before Seni's trackers rescued her?

For now, I hug Nakai, Etana, and Makeda, and I thank the stars we are all safe.

I lead them to the Great Hall where a banquet has been prepared, and I ask them to eat whatever they want. Now that I'm in charge, they'll have only the best.

I've been thinking of how to let Makeda know Papo had died. My other sisters knew what had happened.

After they eat, we take a walk outside and sit on the grass as we watch the night stars. There is no one to tell us we cannot.

"I need to tell you something about Papo." I squat and look Makeda in the eye. "He left for the celestial city of Nahu."

"Is he coming back?" she asks, staring at me with big, innocent eyes.

"No. Once you go there, you can never come back."

She cries softly, and I hold her in my arms until she falls asleep. The next morning, we all hold hands and join a small procession of Sheba's kings as Papo is laid in his beautiful tomb, which he had built while alive. It was in shape of a crouching tiger.

"He was a bad man...but I loved him, and I'm going to miss him," Etana says as she cries on my shoulder.

"It's alright to cry," I say as I wipe the tears from her face.

Our Papo had been a hard man, but we'd loved him. I realise I'm going to miss some parts of him, too, memories from when I was a young girl before I became a woman—I remember his bellowing laughter, the merry songs he sang to his wine cup, the way he flung his cloak and squared his shoulders as he walked around the palace.

As days pass, I find ways to help my sisters get over the gloom of losing Papo. For Makeda, it was horses. I found someone to train her, and she wakes up every morning and runs to the stables. It occupies her mind, and she isn't consumed with grief. Sometimes, I catch her looking at the sky, at the celestial city of Nahu.

As for Nakai, she joined the healers' station for training. She loves helping people and working with herbs, and this is her choice and the path she chooses to take.

"And as for you, my singing dove," I say as I turn to Etana, who is growing taller hour by hour.

She is taller than I am now. "You can sing in the Great Hall, you can sing at the lesser hall, the judgment hall, in the fields, you can sing anywhere you want at the top of your voice." I pinch her cheeks. "Will you sing at my coronation?"

"Yes, I will. Thank you, sister," she says as tears well up in her eyes.

"Anything for you, my songbird." I smile.

I wonder how Sahara is doing. She is a wise woman, and I know she will be fine.

As for Kaku, I finally assign Neret to her, to ensure she eats on time and takes care of her as she continues being the wonderful midwife that she is.

"She can be stubborn, so I need you to be brave and to be firm, make sure she has everything she needs," I say as we walk down the hall to Kaku's room.

"I won't let you down, Empress," Neret vows.

Empress. That's who I am now.

I undergo my training, as well. I love that it's by Seni. He teaches me how to command an army now that I am in charge of one. Ten thousand soldiers remain in Sheba's army, and I'm now their leader.

Apart from that, there is a lot to be undone. A lot Papo had done. I release the kings of Sheba to go back to their kingdoms, to their seats of power, from where they will rule their empires. They choose to wait until after my coronation.

Then there is the matter of the empires he'd conquered. The loot he'd taken from every one of them is returned. He'd robbed the empires blind.

"It's a lot less than what was stolen from Aksa. I'm sorry," I say as I present five chests of diamonds to Seni. I apologize, and I mean it, and I know I have a lot of that to do, on behalf of Sheba to all the empires of the highlands.

He opens one of the chests and takes a diamond out, surveying it in the air. "You keep it. Consider it my gift to you."

"I can't take that," I say as I shake my head.

"Why not?" he asks as he sets the diamond down.

"Because...of how they were acquired, by spilling of blood," I say, walking out of the room.

I need fresh air, so I go for a walk towards the west gate. I'm frustrated. I don't know what's wrong, but I've been in a bad mood all day.

"Fine," Seni says as joins me. "I understand. I'll gift you something else."

I stand near the thicket of trees surrounding the gate. I twirl his locks in his hand and pull him down for a kiss. His forehead and cheek kisses have turned to torture lately. That's why I'm in a bad mood. I kiss him again on his lips, testing. He kisses me back.

He kneels, and his head disappears under my blue robes. I feel his warm tongue on my sex, and my toes tingle.

"You taste so sweet," he says as he moves his tongue luxuriously up and down my sex until I come.

When I'm back to my senses, he takes my hand, and we walk back to the palace before the guards come looking for us.

Seni does not say a word as we go up to my room.

"Empress." A guard greets me as we pass him on his way down the stairs.

I smile and keep a straight face. An hour ago, I was in the fields with him as he taught me, as a child of the household of the archer, how to shoot arrows. I'm terrible at it.

Once we get to my room, Seni kisses me, and I can taste myself on him.

"I'm yours. Use me as you like," he says, taking off his purple robes.

I run my hand up and down his majestic, long, thick sex. It's hard yet smooth to the touch, like velvet.

Starved, I push him to the bed. He falls backwards with a wicked grin on his face as I take off my dress. Crazy with need, I'd forgotten about the two angry scars on my belly, where I'd been shot. Shebiku said they would fade, but they'd take longer because it was a deep wound. I look down on them and put my hands around them.

Seni pulls my hands away. "You are beautiful, every part of you. Inside and out. Now please do as you wish with me."

The need in his raspy voice sent jolts down my body. My hunger reaches its peak levels. I slide down on him, my creamy wetness coating him, my tight sex clenching around him. When all of him is buried inside me, I pause, and we groan in unison.

"That...feels divine." His hands squeeze my ass when I start moving.

"Seni," I call out as I see stars in my eyes as we both come.

And then as I lie down beside him, I realise my mood is lifted.

Chapter Thirty-Five

The next day, I'm watching Makeda train with the horses when a guard comes up to me.

"Dalia and Nasou are here to see you."

I head back to the throne room where Dalia stands with Nasou. He is holding her hand, and they stand very close together, as if attached at the hip.

He discreetly puts his hand on her belly and quickly moves it away. Dalia runs to me and hugs me. A guard steps forward, and I signal him to stop.

"Empress now! You don't know how happy I am. You are going to make a great empress."

We stand outside the throne room, and we both look at Papo's throne. I still call it Papo's throne, as mine hasn't been made yet. I don't know what I want it to look like. I want to change everything in this room. No matter how much the servants scrub it, it still smelled of wine and blood. It reeks of Papo.

I smile looking at the both of them. I'm glad they have each other, and they can be together now, free to love each other in private and in public.

"Empress, I'm here, we are both here—" she takes Nasou's hand, "—to pledge our allegiance to you. We pledge ourselves to your service in any way you need us."

"Thank you, Dalia." I look at the two of them. "You are free to do as you wish with your life. If you choose to go back to Suwi, you have my blessing. If you wish to stay and be of service to me and the empire, then I will be honoured, and I will give you a piece of land where you can build your home and raise your children."

"Thank you Empress. We chose to stay and be of service to you." Dalia bows, and Nasou follows.

It's so formal, I almost laugh.

"Thank you, Empress," Nasou says. He stays behind to chat with the palace guards as Dalia and I head back to Makeda at the training field.

"I could use someone to help me look my best at all times. I need your help and expertise." Now I'm empress, I'm expected to look good at all times. I'm not great with choosing fabrics and taking care of my body and skin. I overlook such things, and Dalia will be of great help to me. Also, I'm no longer afraid of embracing my femininity.

She covers her mouth with her hands.

"You would give me such a position?" Her eyes are wide with shock.

"You are more than deserving." She is good at it. I wonder what she'd do if she ever saw the fabrics in Aksa, and how quick it is to make a garment.

"I will not let you down. I promise on my unborn baby's life," she vows.

"I noticed. When did that happen?"

"Before Nasou left for Aksa. We didn't know it yet, but I was with child." She smiles.

"You will make a great mother." I smile back at her. I wonder if there is a chance Papo could be the father. I hope not. Also, Dalia is an intelligent woman. I'm sure she used the right precautions with him.

"I remember you were here as the uprising happened. How did the war end? Is Hemi alive?" I ask as I wave at Makeda. Seni has joined her in the fields with his stallions, and they are about to race.

Dalia had been left behind when we left for Aksa, so she knows everything that happened.

"When the grand emperor returned to Sheba, Hemi fled back to Astabara, but he vowed to be back."

I knew he'd be back, and I'd be waiting for him.

"The grand emperor's men executed a lot of people because of the uprising. Eight hundred people were captured by the armies and killed. He was in a hurry to return to Aksa, so he had people rounded up and killed, without wanting to know if they were innocent or not," she says as she shakes her head.

Papo had come to Sheba to fight the uprising, then he'd gone back to Aksa, and Seni had pushed him and his mage out, then we'd met at the ultimate battle, where I'd faced him.

"So, you are a Star Summoner. When did that happen?" Dalia asks.

"I don't know." I sigh. "All I know is that it happened, and here we are now."

Chapter Thirty-Six

On the day of my coronation, all the emperors of the highlands and their royal families are in full attendance. I didn't think they'd come considering all Papo had done. I'd expected them to decline the invites, and I'd have understood, but they all came.

We are in the throne room, and King Mesati places a gold crown on my head, and King Wosasi gives me a heavy gold sword that Seni sets aside for me. He is standing by my side.

The kings of Sheba kneel as I sit on the throne, and it is done. I am the Empress.

The emperors of the highlands are the first to come inside and congratulate me.

"Should we tell her about the king-to-king prayer?" Emperor Pesi asks the others.

"Eeeer…" Emperor Gedi scratches his beard.

Seni is sitting beside me. He looks breathtaking in his official purple robes. I can't help but steal a glance now and then. He is not wearing a single diamond. Now that there has been a mass memory wipe, people have forgotten what Aksa looks like beyond its new walls.

"What is the king-to-king prayer?" I ask.

"It's said by a king or emperor to the King of Nahu city, and you can only say it once and your request will be answered," Emperor Pesi says.

I wonder what Papo's prayer was—it must have been something sinister. I guess I'll never know.

"But she is only a woman," Emperor Gedi argues.

From how they've been eyeing me today, I feel like they'd rather be content with a power-hungry emperor like Papo than deal with a woman with power.

"Careful, Emperor," Seni warns as he stares at Emperor Gedi. "She is the empress of Sheba. You will treat her with the respect she deserves. Now tell her about this prayer you speak of."

"My apologies, Empress," Emperor Gedi says.

He goes on to tell me about the prayer, but I do not hear a word he says as I'm too aware of Seni, his liquorice scent flooding my senses. Before we came, he'd gifted me the hundred-and-one diamonds, and Dalia had helped me put them on my skin. Once the ceremony is over, I'll let him take them off me, this time with his mouth. I blush.

As if reading my thoughts, Seni links my hand with his, and I relax. Emperor Gedi, who is finishing his speech on the prayer, looks at our hands and then back at Seni with an approving glance.

"You know the other emperors approached me in the Great Hall last night and asked me to distract you from any ambitions you might have of conquering the highlands. They are afraid you might use your star summoning gift to finish what the grand emperor started," Seni whispers.

"I can't blame them, really."

"They said I should do all I must to distract you. I'm their sacrificial emperor." He sighs.

"Oh, it must be really hard for you." I smile and roll my eyes. "But now that you mention it, I know of ways you can distract me."

"Here?" He looks around at the full room as a princess from Nagarim approaches to greet me.

"Hold on to your pants, Emperor. Meet me in the spice barns after the ceremony is over, and don't be late."

He grins, and before he can answer, there is a loud murmur in the room. I look across to see a man wearing a black cloak standing at the entrance of the throne room. People make way for him as he heads towards me. His glowing eyes settle on me.

"Star Summoner, my name is Tesfaye." He removes a scroll with glowing symbols from his robes. "The stars say this no longer belongs to me. It will help you when the others come."

"When who comes?" I look at the scroll now in my hands. I'm not familiar with any of the glowing glyphs on it.

"You can summon the stars. A lot of powerful mortals and immortals are coming for you. Some wish to kill you, others to use you. Be especially aware of the one who was once light but embraced the dark," he says before he turns and leaves.

I look at the scroll in my hand.

Cursed stars. I have a lot going on right now. Immortal enemies, this is beyond me. I didn't wish for this star-summoning gift in the first place. But isn't that the whole idea of a gift? That you do not anticipate it?

"Look at me. Whatever comes, we will face it together," Seni reassures.

Chapter Thirty-Seven

We are in the spice barns and have snuck away as the others celebrate in the Great Hall. Seni's shock as he sees the diamonds in swirling patterns all over my skin is worth it.

"You know, back in the tent, I almost went crazy when I saw these on you," he says as he traces them on my thighs.

"These are for you to remove later. Right now, I need something fast. We don't have time. They are waiting for us back in the hall."

"Say no more, Empress."

He bows, and I laugh.

Five minutes later, I turn around as he ensures every part of my gown is presentable.

"You know, I think from now on, we should be spending half the year here in Sheba and the other half in Aksa," he says.

"What are you saying?" I ask as I remove a piece of lemongrass from his robes.

"Nila, in case you haven't noticed, I'm in love with you. I've always been in love with you." He tilts my chin, and I look up at him. "Marry me, Nila. I don't want to spend another day without you by my side. I'll be your pillar of strength, and you'll be my refuge. Let's rule together side by side. What's an emperor without his empress?"

His hands hold on tight to my waist.

"Seni, I-I love you…I will marry you…but not now. I need time. Can't we be just friends for now?" I free myself from his grasp.

I want to be with Seni more than anything. I love him, and his proposal tugs at my heart. But apparently, with this star summoning gift, I've inherited enemies, powerful enemies, and that's according to Tesfaye who never lies.

I know Seni assured me we can face anything together, but he has already lost enough because of me. He is just rebuilding Aksa now. Who knows what these powerful enemies will do, what harm they'll cause him? I'd never forgive myself if I put him and Aksa in trouble again. I'll deal with the oncoming threat alone, and when I'm done, I'll marry him.

He steps out of the barn and then looks back. There is pain behind those honey-coloured eyes. "You know I can never be just friends with you, Nila."

The next morning, he bids me farewell as he is returning to Aksa. He was to stay a few weeks after my coronation.

I'm so used to his presence and his assurance, I don't know how I'll cope without it.

"I'll see you in eight weeks," he says as I walk him to his stallion.

He still wants to teach me everything he knows about ruling so I can be more confident in my new status.

"I'll see you then, Seni."

My voice cracks. I feel a lump in my throat. He's about to leave. He wraps his hands around my waist and pulls me against his body.

He leans down and kisses me, teasing me with his mouth as he moves slowly and then fast. When he moves fast, I match his pace. When I do, he slows down and takes his time. I follow the cue, and he's back to fast again. I'm breathless and frustrated.

I caress my burning bottom lip with my thumb as I watch him ride away on his stallion.

He'd made his point clear; we can't be just friends. Friends do not kiss each other like we just did.

Chapter Thirty-Eight

Four weeks after Seni leaves, I take a diplomatic visit to Bazina. This is part of my plan to mend Sheba's relationship with the rest of the highlands. After the short visit, and lots of apologizing for Papo's misdeeds, it's time to go back to Sheba.

"Take the south route and head towards Aksa," I command the soldiers as I get into my carriage.

"Yes, Empress."

We ride for two hours until we are met by a barricade of Aksa's archers who have scaled down the wall. I get out of the carriage, and they let their arrows down.

"Empress, we were not informed that you were coming," their leader says as he steps forward.

"I want to see your emperor. It's urgent."

They look at each other. Their faces and bodies are covered, but I don't fail to see the worry in their eyes.

"What's wrong? Is Seni alright?" I ask.

"If you want to see the emperor, then you need to go now. You don't have much time." He signals to another archer who whistles, and a white stallion appears.

"Can you ride?" the leader asks.

"Yes." I look at the stallion. I've been attending Makeda's classes with her, and I've become a better rider because of it.

"Then get on this horse and ride as fast as you can," he says as he helps me get on the horse.

"What's wrong?"

"We don't have much time. Go, Empress. Go!"

I turn forward and ride fast.

Something is wrong. Is Seni sick? But Aksa is an advanced civilization, and they have found cures for most diseases. What could be the matter?

I ride fast, and when I reach the gates, I urge them to open them quickly. When I walk in, I see hundreds of Aksans gathered around the red monument where I'd stood and lured Eshi so he could be carried off by the wings of justice drone.

Seni is standing on the platform, and we lock eyes as I get off the horse and run towards him. The people part way for me. There is not a dry eye in sight—the men, women, and children are crying.

I run until I get to Seni.

"Empress, is everything okay in Sheba? Are you okay?" he asks.

"What are you doing here?" I ask, looking at the monument and the people.

"I used a forbidden weapon, Nila. I let my people use guns. It's an unforgivable crime in Aksa."

"But you did it to save your kingdom and your people," I argue.

"It doesn't matter. Rules are rules, and what type of leader am I if I bend the rules to suit myself? I'm the one who suggested we use guns. I'm the one who authorised my people to make them and use them. I'm the one who faces the consequences."

Tears fall down my face as I look at him.

"But that means—" I take his hands into mine. "Please don't do this. I'm sure everyone understands."

"We have been trying to tell him the same," Zeli says. She is standing behind me with puffy eyes, leaning against a distressed Kashi. Shebiku stands beside them, grinding his jaw.

"He is so stubborn, he won't listen to anyone," Shebiku says, narrowing his eyes at Seni.

"Seni, you did what you had to do. Everyone understands," I beg, but I can tell he's already made up his mind.

"I'm not above the law. Rules are rules." He has a sad smile on his face as he takes my face in his hands. "You'll be fine. I left instructions that Aksa will always be there to help you in everything you need," he says as hugs me.

I hold on tight to him as I soak his shirt with my tears.

The wings of justice drone floats down, and the cries around me grow louder.

"I love you, Seni. I always have," I say as the drone hovers above him.

"I love you, too, Nila." He caresses my cheek with his thumb as the drone hovers above him and extends its hands. His eyes remain on me as it takes him up.

I fall as I watch the drone fly higher and higher. My heart shatters into pieces. I know it's too late, but I cross my hands over my chest for the king-to-king prayer. But I don't remember any words I'm supposed to say, so I say what I feel inside me with earnestness.

I hear a whooshing sound, and so does everyone else around me. We watch the skies as a black object flies fast across the mountains. Then I hear a rumble as Seni drops from the skies, crashes, and rolls a few feet from where I and the rest of the Aksans stand.

I run to him and help him up. His hands are bruised and bleeding from the landing, and so is his face, but he is alive. He is alive.

I kneel and hug him.

"What happened?" Shebiku asks as he checks his head.

"One minute, I was dropping down the dark hole. The next, something or someone picks me up and drops me here," he says.

"Someone?" I ask.

"Whatever it is, those were definitely human arms," Seni says.

Chapter Thirty-Nine

When Shebiku determines that Seni is all right, we head back to his home and flop on the couch together.

"What a day it has been." Seni sighs.

I punch him on his arm. "You almost died."

I close my eyes as I place my hands over my head. He'd be gone by now. I thought I'd never see him again.

"But I'm here now. I don't know how, or why, but I am."

He sits up and takes my hands. I open my eyes as he kisses my knuckles.

"How did you find out about today?" he asks, massaging my fingers.

"I didn't know. I was coming to see you."

Then I'd seen him on that monument, about to fly to his death.

I sit up. "I was coming to tell you that I missed you, Seni. I missed you very much. I've been in agony since you left Sheba. I love you, and I'm not afraid anymore. I would like us to be more than friends. I agree to become your wife."

"What were you afraid of?"

"Of putting you in danger. Tesfaye said I've made powerful enemies with this new gift. I don't want to put you and Aksa in danger again."

He tilts my chin up. "I can take care of myself, and I want to be with you no matter what. I love you."

He links his forehead to mine.

"Yes," I whisper.

He gently pushes me back on the couch and straddles me. He looms over me like a predator on the hunt. "It's been a month, Nila, and I'm starving."

He kisses me on the neck, and I curl my toes.

"You almost died. We shouldn't," I argue as I angle my neck so he doesn't miss a spot.

"Almost dying made me hungrier. I might need a week before we get out of here." He grazes his lip on my earlobe. He groans, and I arch my back as the sound travels through my body.

"A week? What...what about food and...and water?" I swallow.

"Don't worry, Empress. I'll feed you, and I'll quench your thirst."

Chapter Forty

Five hours later, I stir and wake up from our post-coital nap as the sun sets. Seni is still fast asleep with his hands tucked behind his head. I tuck the stray locs on his face behind his ear.

I leave my warm spot next to him and put on his purple robe. Its three sizes too big, but I love how it smells like him. I stand near the window and look outside, stare across the mountain. I feel thankful for this season in my life. Seni is alive. Aksa is safe. My sisters are happy and protected— they'd live the lives of their dreams. They'd be free to make choices on their own, and I am an empress. I have the power to change lives for good. I'd do my very best.

A strong wind blows against my face. It is so harsh, I cover my face with my arm.

"Star Summoner."

I hear him before I see him. His voice sounds cold, like a sharp whip landing against my skin. I see the enormous black wings first as he descends and stands mid-air over the pool. I peddle back inside the room. His angry eyes look like they are ready to incinerate me.

I don't know what he is, but he is not made of flesh and bone. He might look human with his shining dark brown skin, but his features are too perfect. It's like everything was measured with meticulousness, especially his sharp jawline.

"I do not appreciate being summoned by a mortal." He does not move his lips, but I hear every word, and the annoyed tone in his voice.

"I did not summon you," I reply in my head. I look behind me, Seni is still fast asleep.

"I would not be here if you did not summon me to save him."

He sounds disgusted when he says the word summon. I take a step back when his wings enlarge.

"You have to get me back," he orders.

"Back where?"

"To Nahu."

"I don't know how to do that. Can't you do it?" I gesture at his spread-out wings which now hide the sunset from my view. Can't he just fly back?

"You summoned me, so only you can send me back. I did not make the rules. You have three days, Star Summoner."

He looks me up and down. When he flies down, his boot touches the curve of the diamond where the pool is. It cracks. I thought only a diamond could break a diamond.

"Three days, or I'll drop your male back in the hole I saved him from."

He flies off. The wind that follows his departure is so strong, it knocks me down to the floor with a thud. Seni wakes up and rushes to my side.

Three days? How could I possibly open the gateway to the celestial city in such a short time, or any time at all?

"Are you alright?" Seni asks as he helps me up.

"Yes, I tripped and fell."

He pulls me close and kisses my forehead. "Come back to bed."

I follow him and lay my face on his chest.

"You never told me the answer to the shepherd's riddle." I want to talk about something else and forget the encounter I've just had.

"I'll tell you on our wedding night," Seni replies with as a sleepy voice, and I hear him drift back to sleep.

I can hear the sturdy beating of his heart, and it reminds me he is here, alive, with me, against all odds. We have overcome every obstacle to be here, and now, I have three days if I want things to remain this way. Three days if I want Seni to live. Three days if I want us to have a happy ending.

Thank you for reading **Nila, Princess of Sheba, Star Summoner book 1 by Mukami Ngari**. If you enjoyed this story, please leave a review on the purchase site.

Other books by Mukami Ngari

Pharaoh's Bed
Beautiful Mess
Be My Valentine Vol 2 Anthology

About the author

Mukami Ngari is from Nairobi, Kenya. She is the author of the critically acclaimed novel, Pharaoh's Bed. She enjoys telling sweet passionate romance and women fiction stories set in Africa. When she is not writing or reading, she enjoys practicing yoga and watching supernatural T. V shows.

OTHER BOOKS BY LOVE AFRICA PRESS

Locked In by Opemipo Omosa
How to Fix a Broken Heart by Bambo Deen
Love Prey by Tidimalo Motukwa
Amber Fire by Aminat Sanni-Kamal
Tapping Up by Kiru Taye

CONNECT WITH US

Facebook.com/LoveAfricaPress
Twitter.com/LoveAfricaPress
Instagram.com/LoveAfricaPress
www.loveafricapress.com

Milton Keynes UK
Ingram Content Group UK Ltd.
UKHW011838120424
441050UK00004B/168

9 781914 226540